ADULTING
101

LISA HENRY

RIPTIDE
PUBLISHING

Riptide Publishing
PO Box 1537
Burnsville, NC 28714
www.riptidepublishing.com

Adulting 101
Copyright © 2016 by Lisa Henry

Cover art: L.C. Chase, lcchase.com/design.htm
Editor: Kate De Groot
Layout: L.C. Chase, lcchase.com/design.htm

ISBN: 978-1-62649-450-3

First edition
August, 2016

Also available in ebook:
ISBN: 978-1-62649-449-7

ADULTING 101

LISA HENRY

This one's for Kal. Damn it, Kal, I wish I'd worked this in somehow:

"How's your head?"
"I haven't had any complaints."

You make the day job a little bit filthier, and a lot more fun.

TABLE OF CONTENTS

CHAPTER  ONE

Nick: *Holy shit dude, u have to help me!*
Devon: *What u do?*
Nick: *Remember how my dad got me this job so I'd "straighten up & fly right" before college?*
Devon: *Yeah . . .*
Nick: *There's a guy at work I want to do things to. With my tongue & my dick.*
Devon: *Dude. TMI.*
Nick: *If I suck his dick on the site I'll probably get fired right?*
Devon: *Dude.*

Jai Hazenbrook is ridiculous. Firstly, there's his name. If Nick were on a quest to return the One Ring to the fiery pits of Mount Doom, Jai Hazenbrook would totally be the hot-as-fuck elf in tight leather pants who could shoot the left testicle off an orc at a thousand paces. Whereas Nick, of course, would be the short hairy-footed guy who liked beer and fireworks and second breakfasts. Even in his fantasy worlds, Nick is a realist.

What? He's been waiting for another growth spurt, okay? He doesn't want to be a giant or anything. He just wants to crack five foot ten, really. Five foot ten feels a lot more respectable than five foot seven.

Nick's been waiting on his growth spurt since he was fifteen. He's eighteen now and starting to think it's never coming. Not that he obsesses about it or anything. He's got much more interesting things to obsess about.

Jai Hazenbrook, for example.

Jai Hazenbrook is tall, fuck him.

(Nick *wishes*.)

He's tall and has features that can really only be described as *chiseled*, if Nick's late-night research into romance novels can be believed. Which they probably can't. Otherwise surely Jai would also wear kilts and be a millionaire, but whatever. He's tall, and he's chiseled, and he has incredible eyes that sometimes can't decide if they're blue or if they're gray, but are usually narrowed in Nick's direction in a glare. A why-the-fuck-is-this-kid-always-staring-at-me glare.

Nick is not always subtle.

Okay, Nick is *never* subtle.

Which is why he's pretty sure he's going to be fired by the end of the week.

Nick's dad got him the job at Grover Construction. Disappointingly, it has nothing to do with the Sesame Street puppet, because Nick totally would have been down with that. Harvey Grover is one of his dad's clients. His dad is an accountant. A *certified public* accountant. It's his life's deepest regret that he's dedicated himself to pecuniary responsibility, and has somehow managed to raise a son who "doesn't understand the value of a dollar." Hence this experimentation with a "job."

Look, Nick likes having a job. It's just Mr. Grover very sensibly doesn't trust him much around the actual construction parts of the construction job. Because power saws and nail guns. So it kind of means Nick answers the phone, and runs errands to the sites and back, and spends as much time as he can staring at Jai Hazenbrook's fucking perfect ass.

It is seriously fucking perfect. It's the sort of ass that should inspire goddamn *poetry*. Nick's not the kind of guy who can write sonnets or anything, mostly because he can't remember how to, but if he happens to have a page in his notebook dedicated entirely to ass-related haikus, that's his business, right?

That ass is so hot.
I would totally hit it.
Yes yes yes yes yes.

Nick's haiku skills are maybe a little rusty too, but at least the sentiment is heartfelt.

When Nick's dad arranged this job, well, of course Nick drifted off to sleep with visions of hot construction guys dancing in his head. The visions, not the guys. The fantasy guys did not dance. They just kind of stood around and struck poses, making their unnecessary abs tighten right up, like they were in a Diet Coke commercial or something. Even then, Nick knew the reality wouldn't be so sweet. There would be no come-hither looks from hot-as-the-sun shirtless construction guys. No. There would be hairy backs and beer bellies and lots of ball scratching but not in a fun way. Nick knows the difference between fantasy and reality.

Which is why Jai Hazenbrook has no fucking place in reality.

Which is why whenever Nick is sent out to the site Jai works on, or Jai comes into the office for something, Nick's brain kind of goes offline. It shuts itself down into a protective coma in case Nick starts believing in unicorns or something. Jai Hazenbrook simply does not compute.

And Nick is totally, absolutely going to suck Jai's mythical elf unicorn dick if it's the last thing he does.

Which, at least as far as his job at Grover Construction goes, it probably will be.

Nick: *Which is hotter? My red shirt or my blue shirt?*
Devon: *Nothing makes u look hot. U have a face like an ass.*
Nick: *Fuck you. This is an emergency!*
Devon: *Red.*

Devon Staples has been Nick's best friend since third grade, when their teacher, Mr. Packer, was such an asshole he seated the class according to alphabetical order instead of letting them sit next to their friends. Well, his whole evil plan backfired, because Devon Staples and Nick Stahlnecker are now, and forever will be, best bros.

Their bromance is epic. Devon even took Nick to prom, which was beyond incredible because he's not even a little bit bi—except for the thing that happened at baseball camp when they were fourteen that they don't talk about. He's just super cool, and gets a kick out of pissing off his stepdad, who is an evangelical Christian and can be kind of a dick. So prom was pretty funny.

Devon is also oddly protective of Nick sometimes. He claims it's because he's three months older than Nick, and therefore the big brother in this bromance. Nick claims it's because he's secretly jealous of any guy who tries to get with Nick, because of complex abandonment issues and uncertainty about his own sexuality. It's probably some weird mix of both, but they've never bothered to analyze it except in a teasing way. Whatever it is, it works for them and it's cool.

Devon, naturally, thinks making "blow Jai Hazenbrook" a life goal is a dumb idea.

"Bro, this is a dumb idea."

Nick holds his phone awkwardly between his ear and his shoulder as he buttons up his red shirt. It's his lucky red shirt. If everything goes well, Nick hopes to upgrade it to his lucky red cocksucking shirt. And it does make him look hotter than the blue. It's a little tighter maybe. It makes his shoulders and his biceps look good, and kind of pulls across his chest when he moves. He can make this work.

"Is it?" he asks idly, turning this way and that in front of his mirror to try to judge how hot his reflection is. Either he's really hot, or he's some kid wearing the wrong-size shirt. It's kind of hard to tell objectively which look he's rocking. "Or is it the greatest idea ever?"

"No. No, Nick, it's not." Devon sighs into the phone. "Your dad is going to be pissed if you lose your job. And also if you get caught blowing some guy—"

"Jai Hazenbrook is not just some guy, Dev," Nick tells him haughtily. "Jai Hazenbrook is a glorious, beautiful, dangerous creature who makes Legolas look kind of plain."

"Dude, you need to stop jerking off to the *Fellowship of the Ring*."

"They could be the fellowship of my—"

"*Nick!*"

Nick gets the feeling he's just scarred Devon for life. Which is only fair, really, because last year Devon got really drunk and confessed he'd had a wet dream about Nick's mom. Seriously? And Devon thinks Nick overshares. Nick still gets creeped out whenever his mom offers Devon cookies. He's always half-afraid the bow-chicka-bow-wow music will start up somewhere in the background and things will get crazy gross.

"It would be cool if he had long hair," Nick says. "And leather pants. Maybe he's got leather pants. Do you think I should ask him?"

"You want to blow some guy you don't even know and ask if he has leather pants? You know you're more likely to end up in a weird sex dungeon than Middle Earth cosplay, right?"

Nick considers the possibility for a moment. "I could totally be into that."

"Dude."

Yeah, Nick could totally be into that. He's looked online. He's seen videos. But he also isn't sure. It's like the time he tried blue cheese. It looked pretty good, and heaps of other people like it, and right up until the moment he put it in his mouth, he was totally keeping an open mind. And then it turned out it tasted like ass. Like Satan's ass. But he hadn't known until he tried it for himself. And how else is he supposed to learn things except by trying them? Kinky shit may be awesome and hot and incredible. It may also be blue cheese. Nick kind of wants to know which one it is.

But that's a life goal for another day.

Today's life goal: blow Jai Hazenbrook.

"You've got this," he tells his reflection, determined to give it some confidence. "You're wearing your lucky red shirt, you look hot, and you're totally going to suck some dick today."

A little voice in his head reminds him this is the worst idea ever.

The little voice is Devon. He's still there. Nick tries to explain how this isn't just some random dick, this could be a life-changing dick, but apparently it sounds better in his head than in actual words, because Devon starts making strange high-pitched sounds like he does when they're watching slasher movies and blood and body parts are flying everywhere.

"Fine," Devon says at last. "But when you get busted, then fired, don't come crying to me about it."

"I won't," Nick promises.

He will. They both know it.

"Good luck, I guess."

"I don't need it, bro," Nick says with way more confidence than he feels. "I'm superhot today. Not even Jai Hazenbrook will be able to resist me."

He manages to believe it almost all the way out the door.

By the time Nick arrives at the offices of Grover Construction, his lucky red cocksucking shirt has a coffee stain on it because the damn barista at the place down the street overfilled his cup. What with that and with Devon's prophecies of doom, Nick almost feels like the universe is trying to tell him that hey, maybe this *isn't* such a great idea. Nick ignores the universe. Fuck it, right? What did the universe ever do for him anyway?

Grover Construction is on Second Street. It shares the parking lot with a dentist's office. From his desk, Nick has a good view of crying children being dragged toward the dentist by their parents. It's sometimes nice, when he's really bored and has already counted the staples in his stapler a dozen times, to know that other people are having a worse day than he is. Nick's job is super dull. He mostly takes care of answering the phone and doing filing, and stapling things. Sometimes the things don't even need stapling, but Nick does it anyway. He makes shiny little railroad tracks along the tops of documents. His record is thirty-eight staples on one thing. Then he picked thirty-seven of them out again because he remembered he was supposed to be professional.

Adulting is hard.

The struggle is real.

Patricia is the office manager at Grover Construction. She's Harvey Grover's cousin. She's forty-six and is lactose intolerant. Nick's not sure why she chose to share either of those things with him. It wasn't like he lay awake at night wondering her age. And it's definitely not like he was going to hold her down and force her to drink milk. Patricia is also a Scrabble champion, at the state level. Apparently there are competitions and everything. She keeps a bunch of second-hand dictionaries on her desk, and brushes up on tricky Q-words during her lunch break.

Nick doesn't have a lot in common with Patricia, but they have totally bonded over their all-consuming lust for Jai Hazenbrook.

"Mm-hmm," Patricia said one day after Jai had left the office, his ass looking extra spectacular that morning. "I would do terrible things to that boy."

Nick gasped. "Do you also want to climb him like a tree?"

"I would make him cry for his mommy."

Which, wow, okay, was maybe a little more intense than anything Nick was thinking of, but more power to her. Nick's not scared of the competition, because firstly Patricia is already married to a firefighter, and hello, you don't get to be greedy like that. Once you bag a firefighter, you've already hit the jackpot and thanks for playing. Also, Jai Hazenbrook is gay. Probably. Possibly. Nick is almost sure he's not just projecting when he gets that vibe. So if anyone in the office gets to jump Jai's bones, it's going to be Nick.

It is *absolutely* going to be Nick.

Nick sits down at his desk and fiddles with his collection of paper clips. Then he checks his email, checks BuzzFeed, and it's still only 9:08? What the hell is that about?

Patricia is down the hall in the little break room, making a cup of tea. Nick can hear her humming to herself. She drinks weird-smelling tea that has bits of things floating in it. Nick is not a fan. Not of the tea, or the humming either. Both are not very office-neighborly. Nick feels his two and a half weeks of employment have taught him everything he needs to know about office etiquette, and he's definitely a better coworker than Patricia. Although she has developed a twitch in her right eye whenever he goes on a stapling rampage.

Ker-thunk. Ker-thunk. Ker-thunk.

Stapling things is fun though, right?

Gross tea is gross.

Gross tea also saves the day, because Patricia isn't back at her desk yet when Harvey Grover turns up, wiping a hand over his comb-over to keep it from flapping up in the blast of the air conditioner. He blinks through his glasses at Patricia's empty desk, the corners of his mouth turning down, and then turns his head slowly. His gaze lands on Nick.

"Ah!" he says, like this is an unexpected delight. Which of course it is, because Nick is awesome, but usually people don't notice. Mr. Grover waves a big yellow envelope in Nick's direction. "Nick, I need someone to take this to the site manager on Jacobsen Street."

Nick leaps up from his chair. "No problem, Mr. Grover! I'll do it straight away!"

The Jacobsen Street site.

Jai Hazenbrook.

Nick's lucky red cocksucking shirt.

Really, there's only one way this can end.

Unemployment.

But also bow-chicka-bow-wow.

Nick races out of the office.

CHAPTER  TWO

Jai is loading bricks into a wheelbarrow when he gets the feeling he's being watched. He claps two bricks together, dust flying, and turns around, even though he knows exactly who it's going to be. Jai's not paranoid, but this happens at least once a day, and whenever else the kid from the office can find an excuse to visit the site.

And there he is now, ducking unconvincingly behind a porta-potty, his face as red as his shirt.

Jesus.

Just as Jai is turning away, willing to pretend he never saw the kid if the kid pretends never to have seen him, the kid reappears and waves awkwardly. "Hey."

Jai slams a brick into the wheelbarrow. "Hey."

The kid seems to take his answer as some sort of invitation, and comes closer. His red shirt pulls tight across his chest as he moves. He's not as skinny as Jai first thought. He chews his bottom lip for a second before he speaks. "So, um, Jai, right?"

Jai brushes dust off his gloves. "Hard hat."

The kid blinks at him. "What?"

"You need a hard hat if you're coming on site," Jai tells him.

"Oh!" The kid snorts. "For a second I thought you were, like, correcting me on your name or something, and I was going to say that Hardhat's a pretty weird name. Kind of dumb, even for a nickname, right?"

Jai raises his eyebrows at the kid. "No, I was saying that you need a hard hat."

"I'm not *actually* coming on site though," the kid says. "I'm just standing here right at the edge of the site."

Jai glances at the steel beams above them. "This *is* the site."

"Is it?" the kid asks. "It feels more site adjacent."

Jai rolls his eyes. "Get killed. See if I care."

"Okay." The kid tilts his head slightly and shrugs. "So, my name's Nick."

Jai knows. He's never asked, but he knows because every other guy on the site makes fun of him because Nick has such an obvious crush on him. The guys are pretty good. They're not total homophobes or anything, but if Nick were Nicole, they'd all be encouraging Jai to hit that, instead of snickering at the idea. They're small-town guys with small-town attitudes, mostly. It is what it is.

"Listen, kid—"

"I'm eighteen," Nick says. "And it's Nick."

"Okay," Jai tells Nick. "And I've got work to do."

Nick flushes. "Oh, yeah, sure."

And yet he's somehow managed to insinuate himself between Jai and the wheelbarrow.

Jai hooks his thumbs through his belt loops. "And I'd really like to get back to it?"

Which isn't exactly the truth, but Jai wants out of the weird kid's space. He's here to work, not . . . whatever Nick is doing. Is it flirting? It's hard to tell. The kid's so awkward that a part of Jai wants to cringe in sympathy. The other part of him would really, really like to escape.

There's always a part of Jai looking to escape. Escape this conversation, escape the grind, escape this small town. He spends his days lugging bricks and dreaming of the world outside Franklin, Ohio.

He's got three months of summer to earn some money, and some blisters, and then he can spend the next nine months traveling. Argentina, this time. Living out of a backpack and seeing the world. Jai's been doing it for years. It's a hell of a lot better than staying in Franklin and working construction all year round. Or worse, becoming a corporate stooge. His mom says he's afraid to settle down. Jai keeps telling her he's just afraid to settle.

"Do you own leather pants?" Nick blurts.

"Excuse me?"

Nick freezes like a startled possum. Then his jaw starts working, but no words come out. His face is scarlet and his eyes are owlishly wide.

"Okay, I'm gonna get back to work now." And pretend this never fucking happened. Leather pants? What the hell?

He moves to step around Nick, and is surprised when Nick reaches out and grabs him. Long, thin fingers curl around his forearm.

"Wait! That was weird. Sorry, that was weird. *I'm* weird. So, um, if you can forget that thing I said about leather pants, that would be awesome." Nick's face is scrunched up, like a toddler refusing vegetables. "But, okay, I'm seriously wearing my favorite red shirt and I would really, really like to suck your dick."

For a moment Jai only hears a strange buzzing in his head. It takes a little while for him to actually parse the words. Because on what otherwise ordinary Monday morning does anyone hear words like that? On what otherwise ordinary Monday morning does anyone *say* words like that?

Nick uncurls his fingers from Jai's arm. He looks at Jai hopefully, and shrugs and flashes him a quick grin. "If, um, if that's something you'd be into?"

For three months a year Jai works hard and saves his money. Goes to bed early and gets up before dawn.

For nine months a year he escapes. He goes bungee jumping and cliff diving and a hundred other crazy things his mother doesn't want to hear about.

These two worlds do not collide.

Until right now.

"Yeah," he hears himself saying, his gaze fixed on Nick's mouth. "I'd be into that."

The porta-potty smells of chemicals and urine. It's hot, and there's not much room. Jai finds himself wedged into the tiny space beside the toilet, while Nick pulls the door shut behind them. Then Nick gets down on his knees.

"Oh, gross!"

"What?" Jai asks. He can't see the floor.

"I think I'm kneeling in pee."

Still, that doesn't seem to dampen Nick's enthusiasm at all, because a second later he's tugging at the fly of Jai's jeans, wrenching at the zipper. Jai's tool belt, slung low around his hips, gets in the way. Jai tries to unfasten it, and only succeeds in smacking Nick in the head.

"Ouch."

"Fuck. Sorry."

Nick rubs his head and grins up at him. "It's all good."

Jai hitches his tool belt up, and Nick attacks his fly again. This time he gets the zipper down and shoves his hand straight into Jai's open jeans. Jai's hard already—not fully—but he's getting there fast, and the gasp that Nick gives sounds a lot like one of appreciation. Then Nick's peeling Jai's underwear down, licking his lips, and diving right on in.

"Shit." Jai's head falls back and knocks against the wall with a hollow *thunk*. It doesn't hurt. Jai thinks he probably wouldn't feel it even if it did. He looks down at Nick, at the dark head shoved into his groin, at the red shirt pulled tight across angular shoulders. He keeps one hand on his tool belt so he doesn't brain Nick again, and rests the other one against Nick's head. Nick's hair is long enough for him to curl his fingers through, and a little crisp with gel.

Nick sucks and licks his way up the length of Jai's dick.

It's wet, and messy, and Jai doesn't know whether to just go with it or push Nick away because he feels like an overenthusiastic Labrador. He tugs Nick's head back gently.

"Have you done this before?"

"Yes!" Nick says, breathing heavily. "Kind of? I've watched a lot of porn. Like a *lot*."

So that's actually a no.

Jai is going to hell, for real.

"Also," Nick says, "I've practiced on stuff. Last week I almost choked on a cucumber."

How is this kid even real? Real people have *filters*.

"A cucumber?"

Nick's eyes widen. "Have you seen those clips on YouTube where people try and make their cats scared of cucumbers?" He screws up his face again. "Sorry. Not relevant. I'll just, um . . ." He leans forward and closes his mouth around the head of Jai's dick.

A part of Jai would really like to ask Nick exactly what planet he's from, but it's hard to concentrate while getting his dick sucked. He moans and drops his head back against the wall again.

Nick runs his tongue under the head of Jai's cock, and Jai goes weak at the knees. "Yeah," he says, tightening his grip in Nick's hair. "Yeah, right there."

Nick gives a pleased little hum and does it again.

Jai closes his eyes. It's hot inside the porta-potty. A bead of sweat trickles down his spine. Jai shudders and forces himself not to try to thrust farther into the kid's mouth. Nick wraps his warm fingers around the shaft of Jai's dick and mouths eagerly at the rest of it. He swirls his tongue around the head, then leans forward to take more in and *sucks*.

"Shit." Jai gasps and twists his fingers in Nick's hair.

He's close. It's been a while since he's done this. Last time . . . When was the last time? Yeah, that's right. It was with Gemma. Cute girl from Scotland. A shared dorm room in a hostel in Hanoi, and a shared bottle of Sơn Tinh. She'd blown him, and he'd gone down on her until his mouth and tongue were numb. But a lot of that had been the Sơn Tinh. It'd taken ages for her to come. The next day they'd shared a shower and gone their separate ways. Ships passing in the night and all that.

Nick pulls off him with a *pop* to suck in a lungful of air. His face is red. "'S'okay?"

"Yeah." Jai resists the urge to shove his face straight back down. "I'm getting close."

Nick grins. "Cool."

He dives in again.

This time Nick's more confident. He digs his tongue into the slit, almost driving Jai up onto his toes. Nick makes a small, happy sound and sucks again, which is all it really takes for Jai to start coming.

That's when things happen fast.

Jai's still coming when he hears the sudden bang of a fist on the door.

Nick pulls back with a surprised noise, and gets a face full of cum.

"Shit. Shit. I'm sorry!" Jai hisses, and in the same moment realizes that the crack of light around the edge of the porta-potty door is suddenly getting bigger. A lot bigger. "Fuck. Did you lock the—"

The look on his foreman's face as he wrenches open the door and catches them is one that will probably haunt Jai forever.

It takes thirty seconds for Jai to lose the job he really needs.

He's so eager to get the hell off the site that he leaves his lunch pail there. He's halfway home before he remembers it, but fuck it. He's not going back.

He didn't even bother to try to argue with the foreman. Just walked off the site, leaving Nick sitting on the sidewalk while the foreman called Mr. Grover. Nick looked pale and sick, like a kid sitting outside the principal's office. Jai was worried enough to stop for a moment, and Nick looked up and shot him a wry grin, and shrugged in the universal gesture for what-can-you-do. Well, you could not offer to blow random guys on your boss's dime. Not that Jai isn't shouldering his share of the blame. He didn't have to say yes.

So he left.

Walked down the street to where he'd left his bike, started it up, and ignored the rattling sound that he thinks is the cam chain. He doesn't have the money to get it fixed at the moment, and, oh yeah, now he's also unemployed.

Fuck.

Jai rides out of town, taking the back roads, because the idea of heading home to an empty house is not one that appeals. Nothing in Franklin appeals. It's why he was so eager to get the hell out straight after high school, and why he only comes back for three months a year. It's home, but it's too small-town. Whenever he's back, he's itching to be gone again. A part of him wants to get on the interstate and just keep riding until he hits somewhere new.

Instead, he turns around and heads back into town. He goes to the river and parks up by the entrance to the trail. It's not quite 10 a.m., too late for most morning walkers or cyclists, so there aren't too many people about. He watches the river for a moment and almost wishes he had his lunch pail with him. He's unemployed. May as well enjoy a fucking picnic.

He walks down to the riverbank and thinks about all the time he spent here when he was a kid. His dad loved the river. He used to come here every morning and cycle miles along the trail. A man as fit as that shouldn't have died of a heart attack at forty-one.

Life is short, right?

Why would anyone settle for anything less than living life to the fullest, when tomorrow they may be dead? Yet, wherever he goes in the world, he sees people stuck in the daily grind.

He sits down under a tree.

He feels out of place here, and more so than usual. He's still wearing his damned tool belt. He leans back and unfastens it and lays it on the ground beside him. Wipes his hands on his jeans and thinks of Nick going down on him. His enthusiasm, and his grin, and the way he sucked harder when Jai started to come.

His dick twitches, like it hasn't already seen enough action today.

Farther down the riverbank, a man's throwing a stick into the water for his dog. The dog leaps from the bank and lands in the river with a splash, already paddling.

Jai starts to laugh, and he's not even sure why.

Crazy day.

Crazy kid.

Crazy fucking world.

Mostly, he thinks, he's laughing because he's going to have to explain to his mom why he just got fired.

CHAPTER  THREE

C hris Stahlnecker is not a bad guy. As far as dads go, he's pretty
good. He's not an asshole or anything, he's just a little bit
distant. And not distant in the way that leaves Nick with complex
abandonment issues and a pathological fear of rejection, like Shinji
in *Neon Genesis Evangelion*, just that Chris and Nick don't really
have much in common. Sometimes Nick thinks his dad isn't a dad so
much as he's an acquaintance Nick's been rooming with for the past
eighteen years. Apart from the occasional "straighten up and fly right"
lecture—lectures that Nick politely listens to and then completely
disregards—his dad may as well be a stranger.

Right now, Nick is betting he wishes he were.

If it was about anyone else, Nick would have loved to hear Harvey
Grover explain over the phone to his dad why Nick was no longer
employed at Grover Construction. Because how hilarious would
that be? Except it turns out it isn't funny as much as excruciatingly
embarrassing. Because there is a huge, *huge* gap between Chris
Stahlnecker being okay about the fact that Nick is gay, and having
Harvey Grover hit him with a visual he doesn't need. There is no way
Chris wants his face rubbed in it.

Rubbing his face in things is Nick's specialty.

"He . . . he *what*? Oh my God. Oh. Oh my God." With every
passing second, Chris's face grows whiter. And he was already pretty
white to start with. "Thank you, Harvey. Of course I understand.
Good-bye."

"What?" Nick's mom asks. "What's going on?"

Nick's parents have him trapped in the kitchen, and Nick is a
little bit worried that if he attempts to leave, one of them will rip his
face off.

Nick sits slumped at the kitchen table while his dad leans on the
counter and stares at him. Chris looks a little manic. One eye bulges

more than is probably medically advisable. One hand claws at the knot of his tie like he's afraid it's trying to strangle him. His other hand still clutches his phone.

"What?" his mom asks again.

"Nick got sacked," his dad says.

Right in the eye, Nick wants to tell him, but no. No, Nick.

"Do you want to tell your mother what happened, or shall I?"

"Um," Nick says, and wonders if *neither* is an option. It's probably not. And he really, really doesn't want to say this, but he really, really doesn't want to make his dad do it either. "I kind of got caught doing stuff with a guy? In a porta-potty?"

"Stuff?" his mom asks.

Chris flinches. So does Nick.

"Um, giving a BJ?" Nick says, and, speaking of BJs, he prays to Baby Jesus that his mom knows what it stands for and he doesn't have to explain. Knows only because she's read it in a book, not because she's ever . . . Oh God. What is *wrong* with his brain today?

"Oh," his mom says and blinks slowly. "Oh!"

And then nobody says anything at all.

Nick wrinkles his nose and stares at a speck of congealed ketchup on the table.

The clock on the wall ticks.

The dog waddles into the kitchen, takes one look at the humans, and skedaddles again.

The clock on the wall continues to tick.

"Um," Nick says at last.

His dad's eye spasms.

"No," his mother says brightly, crossing to the refrigerator and rattling around in it, as in *No, I will not let these clouds spoil my picnic. No, I will not admit the glass is half-empty. And no, my precious little angel was not just caught performing fellatio in a porta-potty.* "No, nobody is going to turn this into a thing. This is not a thing."

Nick's eyes widen as she reappears from behind the cover of the refrigerator door, clutching a wine cooler. She twists the cap off the bottle aggressively and takes a swig. His mom is day drinking. He's broken her.

"It was an accident?" Nick attempts.

"An accident?" Chris huffs out. "An *accident*? You *accidentally* gave someone a blowjob?"

If Nick never hears the word "blowjob" come out of his dad's mouth again, he'll die a happy man.

"Um," he says, because, really, what else can he possibly say? "Sorry?"

His dad's face turns a startling shade of red. "Go to your room, Nick."

Nick bolts.

Nick: *I got fired.*
Devon: *SERIOUSLY?!?!?!?! :-o*
Nick: *I feel bad.*
Devon: *??*
Nick: *He got fired too.*
Devon: *Dude.*
Nick: *IKR?*
Devon: *Dude.*

Nick will probably be grounded until he's dead of old age. His dad hasn't calmed down enough yet to say it, but Nick won't be surprised. He lies on his bed and works on his web comic. He's been drawing it since he was fifteen. He has three hundred and twelve subscribers. He would probably have more if he could, like, actually draw. Even after three years his characters look a little lopsided.

It's dark when Devon climbs in his bedroom window, bearing a pizza.

"I *love* you," Nick tells him fervently, and attacks the pizza.

"I know," Devon says smugly, and Nick doesn't know if he's quoting *The Empire Strikes Back* or just being a dick. "So, tell me everything." Then he shudders. "Well, not *everything*."

"I blew Jai Hazenbrook in a porta-potty and we got busted," Nick says around his mouthful of pizza. "Then we both got fired."

Devon winces and flops down on Nick's bed beside him. "Sucks, dude."

Nick rolls his eyes.

Devon winces again when he realizes what he said. "You know what I mean."

"Do I?" Nick asks. "Or are you secretly an asshole who got me a meatlovers with extra sausage just for a cheap laugh?"

"I got you a meatlovers with extra sausage because it's your favorite," Devon tells him, and reaches over to steal a piece of pepperoni. "Is your dad pissed?"

"Totally. Also, he can't look me in the eye, which is weird."

Devon sighs. "Sorry, bro."

Nick knows there will be plenty of time later for Devon to remind him that he told him so, but the cool thing about Devon is that he knows now is not the right time for that. Devon always has Nick's back when he needs it. Devon is the first person Nick came out to. Nick was sixteen. And Devon was totally not surprised. Which, after that thing at baseball camp, okay. Yeah, maybe Nick had totally initiated things and Devon had just gone along with it when Nick promised that straight bros jerked off together all the time. Really, Nick isn't sure why it took him another two years to come out to Devon. And then, when he did, Devon had only nodded, hugged him, and asked him if he wanted backup when he told his parents. Devon is fucking incredible, and, if he weren't straight, Nick would be planning their wedding already.

"I feel really bad for Jai," Nick admits as he chews his pizza crust. "I mean, what if he really needed that job, you know?"

"Um," Devon says. "He's an adult, right? So, like, rent? And insurance and stuff?"

Devon is as vague on the details of adulting as Nick is.

Nick groans. "I'm a horrible person."

"Nick," Devon says, his voice low and serious. "Hey, you didn't force him to do anything, right?"

"Right," Nick agrees, even though it doesn't make him feel any better.

"Remember that time in tenth grade when you asked me if I wanted to pull the fire alarm with you? I didn't *have* to."

Three weeks of detention for disrupting exams. Still totally worth it.

They fist-bump.

"You're not a bad person," Devon says. "You just have terrible impulse control."

It's true. Nick's not even hungry anymore, but he's still shoving the pizza in his face. And he's going to keep doing it until there's none left or his stomach explodes, whichever happens first.

"I do," Nick agrees sadly, then decides it's time for a change of conversation. "How's it going with Ebony?"

Ebony is the girl Devon's been crushing on for almost a year now. They work together at the pizza parlor. Nick's rooting for them, because Ebony seems really cool, but mostly because if they get together, he's going to call them Debony. Or Devony. He hasn't decided yet.

Devebony?

He attacks the rest of the pizza while he listens to Devon wax lyrical about how incredible Ebony is, and how she's funny and smart and also really pretty, except what if she still thinks he helped her make signs to protest the protesters at Planned Parenthood that time just because he was trying to get into her pants? Devon's a nice guy, but he's worried that she thinks he's one of those "nice" guys who's only interested in being friends with her if it goes somewhere. And Devon wants it to go somewhere, even though of course Ebony doesn't owe him anything. It's complicated. Devon's too scared to make a move because he's been crippled by the weight of his male privilege. He only discovered it a few months ago, and it's shaken him up pretty badly.

"Look," Nick tells him. "It's really simple. You ask her if she wants to go out with you, and if she says no, then you still stay her friend."

"But what if she thinks I'm only staying her friend to hide the fact that I want to be her boyfriend?" Devon asks. His eyes go big. "I don't want to turn into one of those assholes who gets all angry on Reddit about being friend-zoned and hates on every girl for being too good for him."

"I hate those guys," Nick says. "Girls *are* too good for them. So are boys. And also every sentient creature that ever existed. You are not one of those guys, Dev."

"What if I am and I just don't know it? What if living with Lewis has screwed me up? In ten years, I could be married to a Duggar sister, Nick!"

"Oh, please. Lewis isn't *that* bad." Nick punches him in the arm. "But if you want to make certain, lean over and give your gay BFF a big kiss."

"No," Devon says firmly. "Not because I'm being homophobic, but because I know where your mouth has been today, and you probably haven't even brushed your teeth."

"That's true," Nick admits. He rubs his aching stomach.

Devon stays with him until there's nothing but grease stains left on the bottom of the pizza box, then gives him another hug and climbs out the window. The tree rustles as he makes his escape.

Nick sends him a few encouraging texts about how incredible he is and how he should absolutely ask Ebony on a date, then crawls under his covers and tries not to worry about Jai Hazenbrook, and whether or not Nick ruined his life today.

Nick checks to make sure Harvey Grover's car isn't in the lot before he steps inside the office of Grover Construction.

"Hi, Patricia," he says, and gives her an awkward little wave.

Patricia sets down her *Official Scrabble Players Dictionary*. "Nick!"

"Hi."

"You!" Patricia says, and she looks like she's fighting a smile. Then, abruptly, she loses the fight, and a high-pitched giggle escapes her. "Oh my goodness, Nick!"

Nick wrinkles his nose and nods. He can feel his face burning. "Yep, me."

Patricia presses her hands to her ample bosom, like she's trying to contain her laughter. "Oh, you don't do anything by halves, do you?" She lifts a hand to forestall the apology on the tip of Nick's tongue. "Was it good?"

"Um, kind of? I mean, if I got the chance to do it again, I probably wouldn't pick a porta-potty and public humiliation, but he's so hot," Nick tells her. "Like burning."

"He really is," Patricia agrees with a wistful sigh. "I'll miss seeing his ass around here."

Nick sidles up to her desk. "About that . . ."

Patricia raises her brows.

"Can you give me Jai's address? I feel sort of bad about him losing his job too, and I kind of wanted to check in with him."

Patricia looks torn. "Nick, you know I can't give out employee details."

"Sure," Nick said, "but he's not an employee anymore, is he?"

"Nick . . ."

"Please?" He chews his lip anxiously.

From the way Patricia exhales heavily, he knows she's going to cave.

"Fine," she says at last, tapping her fingers over her Scrabble dictionary in a rapid tattoo. "But if anyone asks, you looked it up yourself when you were still working here."

"Of course, sure!" It's totally something Nick would have done, if he'd thought of it.

"Employee records are in the back," Patricia says, standing up. "I'll go get it."

While she's gone, Nick heads over to his former desk. He was only here for two and a half weeks, so he didn't actually have time to make his mark office-style. Still, he loads a few pens he brought from home into the coffee mug with his name on it, and collects his notebook of terrible ass-homage poetry. Then he toys with his stapler, smacking it down so it spits out a series of purposeless staples, their little silver legs clenching on nothing but air.

He drops the stapler guiltily as Patricia bustles out of the back office with a sticky note in her hand. She holds it out to him.

"Thanks," Nick says, and gestures helplessly. "Um, it was nice working with you."

"You should never be entrusted with a stapler again," Patricia tells him frankly. "Good luck at college, and good luck sorting things out with Jai."

Nick takes the sticky note, and tries to feel a little bit nostalgic for his whole two and a half weeks as an officer worker.

No.

Nothing.

He'd mostly been bored.

Although he'd learned a lot of interesting new Scrabble words, so it wasn't a total loss.

"Thanks," he says again, flashing Patricia a smile and heading back out into the sunlight.

Jai Hazenbrook lives on the other side of Franklin. And it's not like Franklin is huge or anything, but Nick's dad confiscated his car, so he's only got his bike. And it's summer and it's hot and Nick is sweating like a bitch before he even gets clear of Second Street. And Nick knows his limitations, okay? He knows that he's short, and he knows that he's got hairy toes, and he knows that he has the sort of pale peaches-and-cream complexion that looks absolutely gorgeous, except in summer. In summer he looks like a half-boiled lobster. Really, if he had any common sense at all, he'd turn around and go home and beg Devon for a ride later.

But Nick's never had any common sense, has he? And besides, he's going to apologize to Jai Hazenbrook, not attempt to seduce him. Right?

He shoves his coffee mug and notebook down the front of his shirt, hunches over the handlebars of his mountain bike, and pedals like the wind.

CHAPTER  FOUR

Jai's sister, Katrina, gives him the side-eye when he stumbles into the kitchen for breakfast. "Aren't you supposed to be at work?"

Jai slumps into a seat and helps himself to a piece of toast from Ronny's plate. "Got fired."

"Hey!" Ronny exclaims, then gapes. "You what?"

"Got fired," Jai mutters around the toast.

"What the hell, man?"

Jai likes Ronny. He's better than any of Katrina's exes, that's for sure. They've been together for three years. Kat's first kid calls him "Daddy," and doesn't that get them some strange looks on the playground? Kat's oldest, Caden, is five now, and he's blue-eyed and blond and so pale he needs to be slathered in sunscreen if he even looks out a window. Ronny's black.

"What happened?" Kat asks, holding out a spoonful of mush to Noah, who's strapped into his high chair. He gums the spoon happily.

Jai opens his mouth to tell her, but then Caden bounces into the kitchen.

"Grandma says if someone doesn't fix the hot water soon, she'll cut some bitch!"

Ronny drops his head into his hands.

"Mom!" Kat complains loudly.

A moment later their mother appears, wet hair dripping down the back of her dressing gown. "What'd I do now?"

"You'll 'cut some bitch'?" Kat says. "Really?"

Janice heads for the counter and drops some bread in the toaster. "I said that to myself! It's not my fault that little people have big ears. Besides, if we're talking inappropriate behavior, maybe you should ask your brother why he's not at work today."

Kat cuts Jai a sharp look, eyebrows raised. Jai glances pointedly at Caden.

"Speaking of work," Ronny says, and glances at the clock above the fridge. "Caden, where are your shoes, little man? We are outta here in five minutes!"

There's a flurry of activity. Jai sits back and lets it happen. Ronny and Caden are the first to leave, Ronny with Caden's schoolbag slung over his shoulder. Their mom heads out about twenty minutes after that, swearing under her breath about running late. It always amazes Jai how quickly she can make the transformation from dressing gown to corporate wardrobe. He can only assume that she ditches her potty mouth somewhere on the drive to the bank she's worked at for the last twenty-two years.

Kat whips Noah out of his high chair and sets him on the floor so he can crawl around while she does the dishes.

"So," she says in the sudden quiet following the family's exodus, "what happened?"

"I got caught getting a blowjob on the site."

Kat's eyebrows shoot up. "You what now?"

"Please don't make me repeat that."

"Oh, jeez." Kat bursts out laughing.

"I know," Jai mutters.

Her smile fades. "What are you gonna do for money now? You know what jobs are like around here."

Jai knows. Few and far between. Argentina is looking farther and farther away.

"I'll find something," he says. "Maybe pick up some bar work, or something else in construction if Harvey Grover hasn't blacklisted me all over the county yet."

"Okay," Kat says. "It's just . . . It might not be so easy."

Jai nods. Money's tight at the moment. Kat's been working two days a week at a hair salon ever since Noah was born, even though she wants full-time hours. And Ronny's still picking up what work he can as a substitute teacher because, despite his qualifications, he can't get a permanent contract. It's why they're still living here, and why Janice is helping them out with money where she can. Jai knows he can't ask his mom for a loan, not when things are already stretched thin.

"I'll find something," he assures her.

"I hope you do," she says, and gives him a sympathetic smile. "You'd go crazy if you were stuck here after summer, right?"

"Right," Jai says, and forces a smile.

Jesus.

So right.

The house is quiet once Kat leaves for work, taking Noah to daycare on the way. Jai finishes the dishes and stacks them neatly in the drying rack, then heads down to the basement. His old childhood room is Caden's now, the walls decorated with Minecraft and Pokémon posters instead of the alternative bands Jai followed in high school. He and his friends hung out in the basement to watch movies and smoke pot back then. Now the basement is his bedroom for three months of the year. It's not too bad, except it smells of laundry soap and is damp all the time. Jai's slept in worse places, that's for sure. Like that hostel in Rome where all the toilets backed up at once and flooded the bathroom with shit.

He sits down on the fold-out couch—still unfolded from last night—and opens his laptop. He checks out a few job-find sites, but there's nothing much going on in the local area. It's no real surprise. Jai's never gotten a job through a job site before. He tends to find work through word of mouth. Construction, yard work, bartending, that sort of thing. He opens a new browser window and updates his Facebook status: *Looking for work. Hit me up.*

He heads upstairs again to take a shower, and his mom wasn't kidding about there being no hot water left. When he gets out of the shower, he hears knocking on the front door.

"Shit." Towel tucked tightly around his hips, water still beading on his skin, he hurries down the hall. "I'm coming! Just a second!"

He wrenches the front door open.

Nick gapes at him, eyes glazing over.

Behind him, on the front lawn, a bike's lying on its side, front wheel still spinning.

Jesus. He's a *child*. At least he's not wearing a backward baseball cap.

"What do you want?" Jai asks.

"Nipples," Nick murmurs with a sigh, then jerks like a landed fish. Bright red and foot-in-mouth seems to be his default position. "Shit. Um, what?"

Jai uses the door to shield himself. "What do you want, Nick?"

"I came to say I'm sorry." Nick wrinkles his nose. "Like, I don't know if you even liked your job or anything, but, you know, bills and stuff, and so . . . Yeah."

Nothing that comes out of Nick's mouth ever seems to be particularly coherent.

"It's not your fault," Jai says, and almost means it.

He steps back to close the door, which is a tactical error because Nick takes it as an invitation to step inside. For the first time, Jai notices he's clutching a coffee mug full of pens and a notebook.

"I, um, I cleared my desk out this morning," Nick tells him, gaze traveling around the hallway curiously. "So, this is your place?"

"No, I just randomly shower here."

For a second Nick's expression is blank, and then he grins. It lights up his entire face. "Ha! Good one, dude!"

Dude?

Nick's gaze falls on a discarded toy on the floor. "Wow! Is that Mewtwo?"

Not for the first time, Jai has no idea what he's talking about.

"You know. Mewtwo?" Nick sucks in a sharp breath. "Holy shit. Do you have *kids*? Are you *married*? Is your hot scary husband going to punch me in the face? Or your hot scary *wife*?"

"Way to jump to conclusions there," Jai says. "No, I'm not married, and I don't have kids. Whatever the hell that thing is, it's my nephew's."

"So you're definitely gay?" Nick asks. "Like, definitely?"

"No. I'm definitely bi."

"And single?" Nick presses.

Shit. Jai probably should have gone along with it when Nick assumed he was married. He has a feeling the kid will be harder to detach than a barnacle.

"Single," he admits. "And not interested."

"Oh. Huh. Um, can I ask why?"

Jai raises his eyebrows.

"I mean, no pressure or anything, but apart from the whole getting fired thing, yesterday was sort of fun," Nick says. "And this is my last summer before college, so that's what, two and a half months? I mean, if you wanted to fool around and stuff for the next ten weeks, that would be something I would be totally down for. Or, you know, up for. Unless that blowjob was really terrible or something. Which, I don't actually know. Feedback would be cool, you know, at some point. Whatever." He squints down at his toes and scuffs his sneakers on the floor.

Jai is the king of bad decisions again today. Because why the hell not? Nick's cute. He'd be cuter if he could shut up at some point, but it's not a deal breaker. And it's ten weeks. Nick will be off to college and Jai will hopefully be off to Argentina. Why the hell not pass the time with a fuck buddy? Or at least a BJ buddy.

Nick looks up again and quirks his mouth. "So, um, you haven't said no."

"Still trying to pick through your word salad."

Nick grins again, color rising in his cheeks. "Yeah, I kinda do that."

"I noticed."

Nick's flush deepens, and he appears suddenly shy. "Sorry."

Jai shrugs. "It's okay."

"I'm just a bit distracted," Nick says, gesturing. "With, um, your towel. And your general hotness."

"Right." Jai tightens his grip on the towel. "I should probably get dressed."

He heads down to the basement before Nick can suggest he shouldn't.

Nick's in the living room when Jai reappears. He's checking out the framed photographs on the bookcase. There are so many photos that it's impossible to read the titles of the books behind them. Most of the photos are of Caden and Noah. When her grandkids arrived, Janice pretty much demoted Kat and Jai to also-rans. There's at least one picture of Jai on the bookshelf though. He was twenty-one, and crouching beside a gravestone in Belgium. His dad's grandfather had died there during the First World War. It had felt like something Jai had to do. To let him know the family hadn't forgotten him.

"Wow, you had incredible hair!" Nick says. "Dreadlocks, man!"

Jai scrubs a hand over his head. He gets his hair buzzed whenever he gets home, but tends to let it grow out when he's traveling. The dreads were a one-time thing though. He picked up lice in Paris three weeks after that photo was taken, and never again.

Nick squints at the photograph. "Where is this?"

"Waregem," Jai says. "Belgium."

"Wow." Nick jams his hands into the pockets of his jeans. "Cool. Do you travel a lot?"

"As much as I can," Jai says. "I work summers, and travel the rest of the year."

"How many countries have you been to?"

"Around forty?"

Nick's jaw drops. "Really? That's incredible!"

Jai raises his brows.

"Dude, I've only left Franklin, like, four times in my life, and three of those times were to visit my grandma in Michigan. The other time was Disney World and Universal Studios in Florida when I was ten, which, cool, but they didn't even have Harry Potter World then." He pulls his mouth down at the corners. "I would totally be in Gryffindor, by the way. I did a test on BuzzFeed. Like, three times until it stopped saying Hufflepuff, but I got there in the end."

Jai's not sure if he wants to laugh or strangle him.

Nick scratches his nose. "So, um, it really sucks you lost that job, I guess."

"Something will turn up," Jai says with a shrug.

"Cool." Nick digs his phone out of the pocket of his jeans. "So, um, okay, I turned up and apologized, and that went pretty well, I think. So now I want to give you my number so you can text me when you want to hook up and stuff." He unlocks the screen of his phone and hands it over to Jai. "So, yeah, just put it in there." He snorts. "Your number."

"You ramble a lot," Jai says, entering his number in Nick's phone.

"Yeah," Nick agrees.

Jai hands his phone back. "So text me and I'll have your number too."

"Okay." Nick flushes again, and shoves his phone back in his pocket. He shuffles his feet for a moment, then edges toward the front door. "Okay, so yeah, text me or call me or whatever."

"Okay. See you around, Nick."

"See you, Jai."

Jai almost laughs when, a few seconds later, Nick comes into view out the front window, punching the air in victory. He even does a weird little dance.

"I can still see you," Jai calls out the window.

Nick freezes like a raccoon caught in a porch light, then very slowly turns around to face the window. He gives Jai an awkward wave.

"Bye, Nick."

Nick reaches down and picks his bike up off the grass. "Bye!"

He rides off without looking back.

Holy *shit*.

Jai really shouldn't keep looking, but he can't help himself. He also should have known better than to open the notebook Nick accidentally left behind, but he's too shocked to castigate himself over that right now. He can't stop turning the pages.

Holy *shit*.

Jai's Ass: A sonnet (abandoned)
Jai's ass is like the most incredible thing
I want to do things to it with my mouth
I look at it and heaps of angels sing
And (something that rhymes with mouth goes here)

He flips to the next page and discovers a limerick.

There once was a man called Jai
Who was the world's most hottest guy
And I'm shit out of luck

If we never fuck
I'll scream, "Why Jesus why Jesus why???????"

Jai can't hold back the laugh that bursts out of him, half amusement and half horror. By rights he should feel outraged . . . but it's also hilarious. Nick is insane. He has to be insane. Who *does* this? More to the point, should this be raising any red flags? Because it's not. As much as Jai tries to imagine Nick as some creepy stalker, he can't. Nick's too . . . awkward? Hopeless? Ridiculous?

Jai flips through a few more pages before he closes the notebook. He carries it, and the mug of pens, down to his basement room. The last thing he needs is for anyone in the family to find it lying around. God knows there's enough blackmail material in it for Kat to use against him for years.

He sits down on the folded-out couch, avoiding that one spring that always jabs him in the spine, and reaches for his phone.

He already has a text from Nick: *Hey, it's Nick.*

Jai saves the number to his contacts.

Jai: *You left your notebook here.*
Nick: *SHIT! DON'T READ IT!*
Jai: *Too late.*
Nick: *JGKWNEIKAFUFAJDSKEKK!!!!!!!!!!!!*
Jai: *You're ridiculous.*
Nick: *Noted. Still want me to suck ur dick again?*
Jai: *Yes.*
Nick: *YASSSSSSS! :D :D :D*

CHAPTER  FIVE

I t's a special sort of torture having to wash the car he's no longer allowed to drive, but Nick does it. He tried to argue that a little bit of mud gave his car character, but his dad very quickly shut that down with a "*Whose* car?" Okay, so his dad had paid for it, but come on.

Nick's parents have left a list of chores he's supposed to finish, and Nick's half-assed his way through most of the list already. He's also supposed to clean the pool, but, if he's honest, that's probably not going to happen. He has more important things to do. Like get on GayTube and study blowjob techniques. Because Jai Hazenbrook is a once-in-a-lifetime opportunity, and Nick is going to not waste the fuck out of him.

He finishes washing the car, and puts the bucket and sponge back in the garage, then heads inside to microwave a Hot Pocket. He drops half of it on the living room couch, encourages the dog to clean it up, and then turns the cushion over to hide the stain.

Afterward, grounded or not, he decides to go visit Devon because he's bored. And also because he's not just waiting around for Jai to text him, okay? Even though he's been in a state of perpetual horniness ever since he got Jai's number.

Being grounded is not that big of a deal to get around. Especially not since both Nick's parents work. They don't know how to use the Find My Friends app on their phones to stalk him, so Nick just diverts the house phone to his cell phone and basically goes wherever the hell he wants. As long as he's home by five, he's golden. Also, he's eighteen. What can they do, seriously? They have to know this punishment thing only works because Nick is going along with it. Or pretending to, at least.

Nick rides his bike to Pizza Perfecto, the pizza parlor where Devon works. Devon is working a lot of day shifts to make some money before college starts. Devon is going to Cedarville, not Ohio State.

It's a Christian college. His stepfather, Lewis, is paying. Nick knows Devon is pissed his dad didn't offer to help him out so he could have gone to somewhere less Jesus-centric, but it's not the first time Devon's dad has dropped the ball. It's kind of his thing. He's a douchecanoe.

Cedarville is only a bit more than an hour away from Ohio State, but Nick's already feeling the first pangs of separation anxiety. How is he supposed to survive without Dev? Hence his spending every day sitting in a booth at Pizza Perfecto, hanging with Devon when there's a break between customers.

Ebony is cool too. She brings him free sodas and doesn't judge him too harshly.

"You and Devon are disturbingly codependent," she tells him as she slides into the seat opposite him.

She doesn't *always* judge him too harshly.

"He's my best bro," Nick tells her. "When I was eleven and my first dog died, he turned up at my house with a sleeping bag and a tortoise, and didn't go home for a week."

"A tortoise?"

"He thought it would help. My mom made him take it back to the pet shop." Nick jabs his straw into his soda, breaking up a clump of ice. "Point is, it's not codependency, it's true love."

Ebony's smile reveals a slightly crooked canine that somehow just makes her look cuter. If Nick were straight, he'd probably be all up in her lady business. "Well, how can a girl compete with that?"

"You totally can't," Nick says, then: "What?" His jaw drops. "You *want* to compete with that?"

Ebony is saved from answering by the arrival of the lunchtime rush.

"You could totally compete with that!" Nick shouts at her.

Devon, behind the counter, sends him a suspicious glare.

What?

If Nick's going to have his best summer ever, why shouldn't Devon?

Nick flashes him a grin and slurps on his soda.

Yes.

This is going to be the best summer ever.

Nick's best summer ever takes a nosedive when he gets a puncture in his bike tire on the way home, and is late. His stomach sinks when he sees his dad's car already in the driveway as he wheels his bike down the street. Clearly the universe hates him.

He dumps his bike in the garage and heads inside. His dad's nowhere to be found. Then Nick realizes the back door is open, and he heads outside to find his dad, still wearing his tie, scooping leaves out of the pool with the net.

"Hey," Nick says. "I was totally going to get to that."

Chris levels a stare at him. "No, you weren't."

He doesn't even sound angry, which makes Nick feel worse. "Dad—"

"Don't," Chris says. "I don't want to hear it." He turns his attention back to the pool, dragging the net roughly through the water.

Nick has no words.

Whatever this is, it's new.

Not . . . not his dad's disappointment. Nick's used to that. It's never actually bothered him much, which he supposes makes him a terrible person, but usually his dad is disappointed about things that really don't matter at all to Nick, like failing a math test, or leaving the milk on the counter overnight, or things going in one of Nick's ears and out the other. Nick's dad totally sweats the small stuff, right? The stuff that doesn't count.

But this isn't disappointment. This isn't a lecture on how Nick needs to stop messing around and get serious. This is something new. This is weariness. This is Nick screwing up in so many ways that Chris is *done*, and Nick didn't even know things were anywhere near that bad. It was just small stuff, wasn't it?

"Dad?" His voice is suddenly shaky.

"I said I don't want to hear it, Nick." Chris slams the net onto the side of the pool so hard that the plastic edge cracks.

Nick goes inside again.

He goes upstairs to his bedroom and closes the door behind himself. He sits on the floor in the gap between his bed and the wall, and tries to process what just happened. He feels like a little kid again. He wants to cry, sort of. Except that would be dumb. It hurts though. It hurts that his dad must think he's so selfish that he doesn't give a fuck about how far he's pushed him, when Nick just didn't *know*. He thought they were okay.

Why didn't anyone tell him they weren't?

His gaze falls on the corner of the pages his mom printed out for him about housing at OSU. It seems just as complicated as the day she presented them to him, months ago now. Like he was supposed to decide where he was going to live from that? And not just shuffle the papers and randomly choose one, which is what he's done. He still hasn't read through them all, but his mom seemed okay with the one he picked, so. He drags the papers out with the toe of his shoe. He stares at them for a while, and then shoves them back.

He's supposed to be thinking about college.

He's supposed to be thinking about what courses he's going to take, and what meal plan he wants, and what to pack . . . And all of this is supposed to make him excited, or something. He still hasn't figured out the appropriate level of enthusiasm to show when his mom drags him to Walmart on yet another expedition to find clothes and storage boxes and sheets and towels.

He just . . . He doesn't even know what he wants to do with his life. Is he supposed to? There are kids he went to school with who totally have all their shit figured out. What school they're attending. What degree they're getting. What career they'll have. How old they'll be when they find their partner, buy their house, and have their kids. Meanwhile Nick can't even decide what to watch on Netflix tonight.

It's weird.

When Nick was a kid, he'd sort of had a crush on Lee, his mom's cousin. Lee was like eighteen or something when Nick was six. When Nick was six, eighteen had seemed very grown-up. Lee had a car and everything. And he was totally hot. Hot in a way six-year-old Nick didn't really understand. He only knew he wanted as many wrestle-hugs as he could get. It wasn't until years later that Nick actually understood what had been going on there. He still hopes to hell Lee doesn't.

Point is, Lee was hot and grown-up and cool, and Nick had figured it was something that happened to everyone. That at some point you got tall and grew out of pimples and into the ability to understand what stock options are. So far, none of that has happened for Nick, and he's starting to worry it maybe never will. Maybe growing up isn't something that just happens organically. Maybe there's something he's supposed to do to make it happen. Like start watching PBS instead of the Cartoon Network? Which actually seems a little drastic, to be honest.

He just . . . There are things he cares about, okay? Like sometimes the world feels like such a shitty place it makes him want to scream, and other times it's so beautiful he just wants to cry. Like last week, when he saw this little kid stop outside the dentist and point out a dandelion growing out of the cracks in the pavement. And the kid's mom stopped too, and they both crouched down over the dandelion and looked at it. Then the phone rang, and when Nick looked out the window again, they'd gone. And all he could think was that if more people stopped and noticed dandelions, maybe the world wouldn't suck so much. But when he wrote it down in the back of his notebook, it had just seemed sort of dumb.

A stab of embarrassment draws him out of his darkening mood.

His notebook. His notebook full of ass poetry that Jai has now seen.

Nick covers his face with his hands and groans.

Okay, so Jai wants to mess around even after reading Nick's ass poetry, which is cool—which is beyond cool, actually—but still. Nick doesn't have a lot of dignity, so he feels it's important to treasure the tiny scraps he has. And now he has none with Jai. Absolutely none.

He takes his phone out of his pocket and goes back through his messages from Jai, just to make sure he wasn't dreaming.

Nick: *Noted. Still want me to suck ur dick again?*
Jai: *Yes.*

Nick likes that yes. It's unequivocal. Solid.

He leans his head back against the wall and closes his eyes.

Okay, so maybe he's really bad at adulting, but at least he's going to lose his virginity before college, right? That's pretty grown-up. Assuming Jai wants to go there, or course. But Nick's watched a lot of porn. He's fairly sure that eighteen-year-old virgins who are kind of good-looking, at least in a favorable light, are in high demand.

And this way, by the time he gets to college, he'll know what he's doing when it comes to sex, right? Like, he won't mess it up really badly and the whole campus will find out, basically.

He hears his mom's car pull into the driveway and then, a few minutes later, the murmur of his parents' voices downstairs.

He tries to imagine them when they were young. Tries to imagine that maybe there was a time in their lives when they did dumb things or almost cried about dandelions too. He's spent his whole life with them as his parents. He wonders what they're like as people. Once, at one of his dad's work functions, his mom got drunk and led the whole room in a conga line. The craziest thing about it was that his dad joined in on the end, and Nick felt like he was watching someone else's parents. Or maybe watching the people they were before they were parents.

It was funny. It was somehow sad too. And scary, maybe, in ways Nick can't quite articulate. Like, does becoming an adult mean losing a part of himself? Or is he just being a fucking teenage drama queen?

Nick hauls his laptop down from the bed and opens it. He goes straight to Facebook and opens up a chat window. Devon's online.

Nick: *I'm scared I'm going to hate college. Or that it's going to hate me.*

Devon: *Me too, bro.*

Nick: *It's like I still don't even know what I want to do with my life but too fucking bad Nick, because you've run out of time and now it's locked in. Like the only reason I picked criminology was because I was watching old eps of Criminal Intent at the time. THAT'S NOT A WAY TO PICK A MAJOR, DEV!*

Devon: *Dude, you can change your major if you want. Your not locked in.*

Devon: **you're*

Nick: *This is FB, Dev. Spelling doesn't matter.*

Devon: *Please, I know you get secretly mad at me when I use the wrong one.*

Nick: *It's true. I do. Because I'm a horrible person.*

Devon: *Yes, that's the reason.*

Nick: *I love you though.*

Devon: *ILY too.*

Nick: *Mostly I love how I can say I love you and it doesn't have to be weird.*

Devon: *You want me to come over and give you hugs?*

Nick: *Always.*

Devon: *See you soon, bro.*

Nick smiles as Devon ends the chat.

Then the smile fades when he remembers exactly how much he's going to miss Devon once college starts.

One thing leads to another, and Nick wakes up the next morning to find Devon stuck to him like a wet Kleenex. The one thing in this case was pizza. The other thing it led to was a *Lord of the Rings* marathon. Nick had fallen asleep during *The Two Towers*, right at the part where Aragorn meets Éomer, and in the middle of that tense standoff, they both completely validate Nick's thing for older guys with beards.

Jai would look totally hot with a beard.

Anyway, Nick wakes up to a gentle knocking on his door and Devon spooning him.

He blinks wearily as his mom peers around the door.

There was a time when Nick and Devon had to swear to his parents that they weren't sleeping together—well, they were sleeping, but that was all—because yeah, they are weirdly codependent and they are snuggle buddies. Nick's mom doesn't even blink these days when she finds Devon sleeping in Nick's bed.

"Breakfast's ready," she says.

Nick elbows Devon awake, then they both stumble downstairs like something out of a George A. Romero movie.

Nick slides into the seat across from his dad at the kitchen table. Devon slumps down next to him.

Nick's mom sets pancakes on the table in front of everyone.

"Thanks, Mrs. S!" Devon says.

Nick's mom gives him an extra pancake. "I've told you a hundred times, Devon, it's not Mrs. S, it's Marnie."

"Right," Devon says, color rising in his cheeks. "Marnie."

Nick shovels pancake into his face. He's pretty damn sure his mom wouldn't be so friendly if she knew about that dream Devon had about her. Which, really, there should be boundaries in this bromance, right? Nobody should have to deal with: *"Dude, I dreamed I boned your mom!"* Nobody.

"Um, Dad," he says, "so I'm really sorry about yesterday. I'll get all my chores done today."

His dad glances up from breakfast. He looks unimpressed. He looks like someone who's heard that a thousand times before.

Guilt stabs Nick.

"Fine," Chris says at last.

"And I was thinking that I could go looking for another job?"

Chris is silent for a moment. Then he stabs a piece of pancake with his fork. "If that's what you want."

Well, no, not really. Jobs kind of suck. But Nick *does* need the money for college. And he'd sort of like his dad to not hate him. "I do. Can I have the car back?"

"If you find a job, you can."

Ouch. But also fair.

"Okay," Nick says. "Thanks, Dad."

He's gratified to see a faint look of surprise cross his dad's face that for once isn't accompanied by disappointment. It makes him feel cautiously hopeful, like maybe if he doesn't screw this up, he and his dad will be okay.

And he wants them to be okay.

Maybe this is what growing up feels like.

CHAPTER  SIX

By Friday, Jai still hasn't found any work, and he's sick of thinking about it. He thinks about Nick instead, and thinks about texting him to hook up. Jai's twenty-five years old and never had a fuck buddy. His hookups are spontaneous and short-lived. He's not sure of the etiquette of arranging these things beforehand. If he texts Nick, what does he say?

Also, Jai would put money on the fact that Nick's a virgin. Jai hasn't been a virgin in years. Sex is casual to him, a natural extension of attraction and camaraderie. Spend a few hours or days with someone cool, and sex is a thing that happens organically, and everyone parts as friends with no expectation of ever doing it again. Sometimes Jai's run into people he's slept with a week or a month down the track, at a new hostel in a new place, and often they've picked up exactly where they left off. But usually it's new faces, new stories, new moments, and new bodies to learn in the small amount of time they have together. It's fun and friendly. It's not a thing that Jai has ever actually scheduled.

But tonight would actually be perfect. Kat and Ronny will be out, and his mom will be watching the kids. And it's not like Jai has any other pressing plans, like beers with the guys from the site.

Still, this feels like a big step. Nick said it was no strings, and that's fine, but even ten weeks is about ten times longer than any of Jai's previous relationships. Jai's relationships usually last right up until someone has to get on the next bus or train or plane. Ten weeks feels like a long time.

Jai stares at his phone screen for a while before he actually texts Nick.

Jai: *Hey.*
Nick: *Hey :)*

God. Again with the smiley faces. Why is Jai even surprised?

Jai: *Are you doing anything tonight?*
Nick: *Sucking ur dick hopefully.*

Jai lets out a bark of surprised laughter.

Jai: *How about you come over and we watch a movie and see where it goes?*
Nick: *Sounds good. What time?*
Jai: *8?*
Nick: *See you then!*

Jai sets his phone down. Okay, so that was easier than he expected. He checks his wallet. He's down to his last twenty-dollar bill and change, but he should probably get some chips and soda.

In the end he walks to the gas station a few blocks away and picks up Doritos and salsa, a bottle of Coke, and a pack of condoms. Not that he's going to pressure Nick into anything, but it's not like he won't use them eventually anyway.

Then he spends the rest of the day cleaning the basement, even though he figures the sort of guy who'll give a blowjob in a porta-potty isn't going to give a damn.

It gives him something to do apart from worry about exactly what he's getting himself into.

But life is short.

The doorbell chimes just before eight.

"Jai!" Janice yells from the living room. "Doorbell!"

"Yeah, Mom," Jai says, heading up the stairs. "I heard!"

Jai's hoping she can keep Caden from heading down into the basement to visit with Uncle Jai. That's fine with Jai most nights, but he really doesn't need Caden bursting in tonight.

Jai opens the front door.

Nick is wearing jeans, a Gryffindor Quidditch Team T-shirt, and a nervous smile. "Hey!"

"Hey," Jai says, and steps back from the door to let him in. "I'm in the basement."

It has to be a testimony to Nick's age that he doesn't even give Jai the side-eye for admitting that. Not that Jai's ashamed of living in his mom's basement while he saves money to travel, but he's used to people looking at him like he should be.

Nick follows him down the stairs.

"So, um, is it weird, like, me coming over when your folks are home?" Nick asks.

"My mom," Jai corrects automatically. "And I'm twenty-five. She quit telling me who I could have over a while back."

"That's cool," Nick says, looking around the basement curiously.

It's not much, really.

There's the fold-out couch, the TV, a chest of drawers and a closet, and a bookshelf. The washer and dryer are up against the back wall. There's shelving up against the back wall too, full of the usual basement detritus: old board games with missing pieces, boxes of Christmas decorations, lawn seed, and, for some reason, four different types of fabric softener. The place looks like the "before" shots on a home decorating show.

Nick pads over to the bookshelves. He shoves his hands into the pockets of his skinny jeans and rocks back and forth on his heels a little as he checks out the books on Jai's shelves.

"Have you, like, *read* Faulkner?" he asks, as though he can't even imagine such a thing. Then, before Jai has a chance to answer, he's off on another tangent. "I thought you'd have more stuff. Like, um, souvenirs and stuff from all those countries you've been to? My grandma had a whole hutch full of porcelain thimbles. You wouldn't think there'd be a huge demand for porcelain thimbles, right, but you can buy them *everywhere*. I mean, do you think there are entire factories somewhere just cranking out porcelain thimbles?" He shakes his head and turns to meet Jai's gaze. "That makes me feel complicated things about consumerism."

"I don't buy a lot of stuff when I travel," Jai says.

"Why not?"

"Most of it's just a waste of money, and it takes up space in my pack, and all it's going to do when I get it back here is collect dust."

"But how do you know where you've been without cheesy novelty salt and pepper shakers to remind you?"

"I take a lot of photos," Jai says. "Sometimes I'll listen to the same music I did when I was in a particular place, and I'll close my eyes and I'm there again."

"Oh. You're like totally Zen or something, aren't you?"

"Do you even know what Zen means?"

Nick's mouth quirks up in a grin. "Something to do with motorcycle maintenance, right?"

If he's making a joke, it's pretty funny.

If he's serious . . .

Well, if he's serious, at least he's cute.

Jai opens his laptop and logs into Ronny's Netflix account. "Anything in particular you want to watch?"

"Um, anything, I guess," Nick says. He bounces on his feet for a moment longer before apparently coming to a decision, and sits down on the couch beside Jai. He's close enough that Jai can feel the warmth of him where their jean-clad thighs are almost touching, but he's keeping a tiny gap between them.

Jai leans over and sets the laptop on the coffee table, shifting a little so that his leg presses against Nick's. Then, when the laptop's set up so they can both see the screen, he doesn't move back again.

They watch *Parks and Recreation*, and Jai learns that when Nick laughs, his face goes bright red and his body sags. He leans more into Jai as he relaxes, and manages to get Dorito dust all over his shirt. And Jai's.

"Are we Netflix and chilling?" he asks.

Jai makes a face. "I don't know what that means."

"Are you twenty-five or are you eighty-five?" Nick asks, eyes bright.

"Whippersnapper," Jai grumbles, and Nick laughs.

When they kiss, Nick tastes like nacho cheese and salsa. Nick's hands settle lightly on Jai's hips, their legs slotting together as they turn toward one another. Nick's a messy kisser, hesitant and eager at the same time, so Jai puts a hand under his jaw and holds him gently in place. Then he moves their mouths together again and licks the seam of Nick's lips until it opens. Chasing down Nick's tongue is a whole other challenge. It's like a frightened little woodland creature that's hiding in its burrow. Jai presses his tongue into Nick's mouth, then draws it back again. He does it three times before Nick gets the hint and finally follows it with his own.

Then Nick sucks in a hitching breath and breaks the kiss.

"Are you—" Before Jai can even get the question out, Nick shifts forward and straddles his lap. He holds Jai's shoulders, his knees digging into the couch on either side of Jai's hips.

They kiss again. Jai chases the now-faint taste of Doritos with his tongue, before pulling back to suck for a moment on Nick's lower lip.

Nick makes a small, surprised noise and digs his fingers into Jai's shoulders. He wriggles on Jai's lap, like he's trying to grind their dicks against each other, but also trying not to. "So did you . . . did you want me to blow you tonight?"

Jai raises his eyebrows. "Maybe I can blow you?"

Nick's wet mouth falls open. "What?"

Jai shrugs. "If you want."

"Oh my God. I *so* want." Nick swallows with an audible *click*. "Like, yeah. I've never . . . I so, *so* want."

It's like he doesn't even speak English.

Jai manhandles him off his lap and leaves him sprawled on the couch. Nick's eyes grow impossibly wide as Jai moves onto the floor on his knees, and shifts forward so he's between Nick's thighs. Nick's jeans are so tight that Jai can see them straining against his erection. He reaches up and unbuttons Nick's fly. Nick tilts his hips so Jai has better access.

The zipper rasps as Jai tugs it open.

"Captain America underwear," he says. "Why am I not surprised? It's like pop culture exploded all over you."

Nick wrinkles his nose. "Can you please not say 'explode' when you're so close to my dick, dude? I'm already on a hair trigger here."

Jai laughs and leans in. He peels down Nick's Captain America underwear, and Nick squeaks and his entire body stiffens. Then his fingers are on Jai's scalp, scrabbling uselessly to find purchase in his buzz cut. Jai laughs again and wets his lips, then hunches over and takes the head of Nick's dick in his mouth.

He's got a nice dick. It tastes like apple bodywash over a hint of sweat and musk, and it's leaking furiously. Nice balls too. Jai rolls them in his palm, hair tickling his skin. Jai has visions of taking his time, drawing this out until Nick's a quivering mess under his attention, of blowing the kid's mind as well as his dick, but—

"Holy shit!" Nick groans, and it's all over with a shudder and a spurt of salty cum into Jai's mouth. By the time Jai pulls off, Nick has a hand over his eyes. "Oh my God. Shit. Oh my God."

Jai's grin dies as Nick tugs his underwear back into place, still keeping that hand over his eyes, and twisting away as he moves. "Nick?"

"Um, yeah." Nick swallows, hitching his jeans up with his free hand. "So, um, I should probably go, I guess. Walk of shame and whatever. Or, you know, walk of mortifying humiliation."

"Hey." Jai grabs his wrist. Gently forces his hand away from his face. "What's wrong?"

Nick's face is scarlet, and he can't quite meet Jai's gaze. "Um, sorry. I'm sorry."

"For what?"

Nick looks at him like he's crazy. "For, um, bringing dishonor on my family name and humiliating every single one of my proud ancestors by coming *instantaneously*? It was like fifteen seconds, dude. I *counted*."

"The first time a girl tried to blow me, I came all over her sweater the second she opened her mouth," Jai tells him, inwardly cringing at the memory.

"Really?" Nick asks, a note of hope in his voice. "Is it one of those things you laugh about now?"

"Yeah," Jai says. "Although she also laughed at the time."

"Ouch." Nick plucks at the hem of his T-shirt and chews on his lower lip for a moment. "So, um, you're not gonna laugh at me?"

"Nope." But Jai can't stop the smile tugging at the corners of his mouth. "It's kind of a compliment, right?"

Thankfully, Nick smiles too. "I don't know. I mean, I'm pretty sure a stiff breeze could have brought me off."

"Okay," Jai says, rubbing Nick's thigh. "I won't get all big-headed about it, then."

"You'd better not," Nick mutters, but his smile grows a little. So does his flush.

Jai climbs back onto the couch and nods at the laptop. "Want to watch another episode?"

"Okay," Nick says, shoulders slumping as he relaxes again. "Cool."

It's midnight before Nick leaves.

Jai takes their glasses and the empty chip bowl up to the kitchen. Janice is pottering around in her dressing gown and slippers, eating ice cream from the carton.

"You're not violating a child, are you?" she asks.

"He's eighteen." Jai sets the bowl and glasses in the sink.

"Jai, I saw him leave on a *bike*."

"He's still eighteen."

"Good," she says. "Because I am not selling this house to mount a legal defense for you."

"Good to know, Mom."

She jams the spoon in the ice cream. "So now we've established I raised you better than that, when do I get to meet him?"

"How about never?"

Janice raises her eyebrows.

He sighs. "Look, it's nothing serious, okay? We're just messing around until he goes to college and I go to Argentina."

"So what? I don't get to meet some boy you're bringing back to the house? I'd like to say hello, Jai, not plan your damn wedding."

"That was never going to happen anyway."

"I know." Janice holds out the ice cream. "You're like your father. Happier alone."

He freezes with his hand outstretched toward the draining rack, fingers twitching over a spoon. "What?"

She shrugs. "Oh, I don't mean he was unhappy or we were living a lie or anything. Just that your dad was an introvert, you know? Like you."

"I'm not an introvert."

"An introvert isn't the same as a shut-in," she says. "An introvert is someone who recharges their batteries when they're on their own, like you, not when they're around other people, like me and your sister. I go mad when I don't have anyone to talk to. You're good on your own. You like it."

Jai snags the spoon and then the ice cream. "I have plenty of friends, Mom."

"You have plenty of friends for very short periods of time," she points out. "Then you pack up and go somewhere else. There's nothing wrong with it. You're just wired differently. When the zombie apocalypse comes, you'll be fine living in your mountaintop cabin with only the birds for company."

The zombie apocalypse? Jesus. His mom and Nick would get along like a house on fire, wouldn't they? That's just the sort of random reference Nick would love. Jai's not sure what worries him most: the fact he's already noticing the things Nick would love, or that he's apparently hooking up with the teenage-boy version of his mom. There's not enough ice cream in the world to deal with a realization like that.

"And in the zombie apocalypse, you would . . .?"

"Die by shooting myself in the head as I was surrounded by a horde of revenants, sacrificing myself after creating a diversion so the rest of you could escape."

"The fact you didn't even have to think about that for a second is incredibly disturbing," he tells her.

Janice shrugs. "*The Walking Dead*, Jai. How have you never watched it?"

"Is it on Netflix?"

"Ronny has it on DVD."

"Maybe I'll borrow it."

"Maybe you should." She drops her spoon in the sink. "And maybe next time your friend is over, you'll introduce me."

He knows when he's beaten. "Okay, Mom."

"Good night, Jai." She smiles, and the wrinkles around the corners of her eyes deepen.

"Night, Mom."

He finishes half the ice cream before he heads back downstairs to bed.

CHAPTER SEVEN

Nick: *Got my first BJ last night!*
Devon: *Congratulations?*
Nick: *Fuck yeah congratulations! Except it was over really fast. :(*
Devon: *TMI.*
Nick: *Seriously though? How long did u last when that Mathlete girl blew u?*
Devon: *HOURS, BRO. HOURS. I was like a machine.*
Nick: *Dirty liar.*
Devon: *:D*

B ecause his parents said he could go to Devon's on Friday night, Nick decides that over the weekend he should really try to get another summer job like he promised he would. He doesn't feel guilty for going to Jai's place instead, but he does feel like since he's totally abusing his parents' misplaced trust, he should at least try to do something right. Also, it'd be nice to get his car back and not have to ride his bike everywhere.

Job hunting in Franklin totally sucks. Nick spends five minutes poring over the ads in the back of the local paper, then gives up and turns to the comics instead. Wow. Not only are newspapers still a thing, but so is *The Family Circus*, huh? Nick then spends ten minutes googling the history of *The Family Circus*, gets sidetracked by a few random links, and then it's suddenly two hours later and he's been sucked down a bishounen rabbit hole on Tumblr.

It happens.

It happens a lot, actually.

Before his dad was obsessed with getting Nick a job, he used to be obsessed with getting Nick a hobby, or a sport, or something, because apparently spending hours on his computer all day or drawing his web comic are not what Chris Stahlnecker considers a healthy use of his son's time. Which is pretty unfair considering Nick inherited his dad's complexion. He's part alabaster, part vampire. The sunlight does not agree with him. Last summer while Devon was getting an even, glowing tan, Nick was peeling like old paint. It was not at all attractive. Also, it itched like hell. So pardon Nick if he much prefers the indoors.

He thinks of Jai working on the site, and how hot he looked, in both senses of the word. Really, Nick's glad Mr. Grover gave him an office job instead of something on the site. Air-conditioning and indoor bathrooms are two of Nick's favorite things.

Thinking of Mr. Grover makes him feel bad. He wonders idly if he should write a letter of apology to Mr. Grover, then decides that he probably should, but also that he probably won't. Because awkward.

Nick eventually heads to the bathroom to shower. When he gets back to his bedroom, his mom is standing in front of his open closet with a notebook in her hand.

"Mom?" he asks warily.

His mom has a calculating look in her eye. "It's only a few months until you're off to college, and we need to figure out what we have to buy you."

Nick's mom loves writing lists. She writes grocery lists and laundry lists and lists of chores for herself and for Nick's dad and for Nick. She writes lists about what she has to do every week, and then breaks them down into daily checklists. Once, when she and Nick's dad went away to a conference overnight, the list she left Nick—which covered everything from remembering to feed the dog to all the emergency numbers she could think of—was three pages long. She writes lists about what lists she needs to write.

"If we get it now, you won't need to dip into your own money once you're at school," his mom says.

Nick has almost four thousand dollars in his college account. It's more money than he's ever seen in his life, and it doesn't quite feel real because it's just a row of numbers on a statement. Nick sort of wants to go to the bank and withdraw the whole lot in one-dollar bills so he can make it rain. But the account is actually in his dad's name, since he opened it when Nick was still a toddler, and his dad won't sign it over yet because he knows Nick too well.

The money is for when he's at college. For incidentals and stuff that his parents aren't going to cover for him. It still seems like a lot, but his parents worry it won't last very long at all. It's a lifetime of saved money. It's twenty dollars here and fifty there. It's birthdays and Christmases. It's from uncles and aunts and grandparents. It's from Nick missing out on splurging on comic books and candy, and forgoing the instant gratification of buying wonderful, glorious *things* in order to have the money for the future.

And now the future is here, and Nick's not ready for it.

Nick sits down on the end of his bed, his stomach knotting.

What he told Devon is true. He's scared of the idea of college, and not just because it means a forced separation from Devon, which should absolutely be against the Geneva Conventions. He's scared he doesn't know what to do with his life, and he's run out of time to decide. He's scared he's expected to be an adult now, and he still feels like a kid. Mostly, he's scared that in a few years he'll look back and not even recognize himself. Nick *likes* who he is, okay? Even if he hasn't totally figured himself out yet. And it feels like college is a non-Nick-shaped box he's being shoved into, and in order to fit, he'll need to lop parts of himself off.

And then, when he thinks about that, he worries he's maybe overreacting. It's just he can't shake the idea that growing up feels a lot like giving in. It feels a lot like losing something valuable, even if that something is so intangible Nick can't properly articulate it. How is he supposed to want to study criminology when it only feels like last week he was eight years old and wanted to be a Jedi?

Everything he was, and everything he is, has somehow been distilled down to this moment. To his mom setting out his balled-up socks in a regimented row on the floor and counting them up, and somehow closing the door on the childhood—on the freedom—Nick's not yet ready to leave behind. It's all socks and storage boxes, and pillowcases and linen, and minors and majors, and for a second Nick feels like he can't breathe properly and will never be able to breathe again.

It's like trying to grab a fistful of water and hold on to it.

Nick closes his eyes and pushes down the sudden spike of panic tearing through him.

"Nick?" his mom says. "Nick?"

He opens his eyes again.

"I said, you're going to need new socks."

Nick blinks down at the row of socks, and feels like he may as well be looking at something he's never seen before. "Okay," he says at last, his head buzzing. "Sure, Mom."

On Saturday afternoon Devon comes over for a swim. He brings Ebony with him, and she brings her friend Shelley. Shelley is only sixteen, but she already has a tattoo. She shows Nick the tattoo, and the fake ID she used to get it.

"I'm telling you, bro," Nick says in an undertone when he and Devon are lazing in the deep end of the pool, "my mom was counting my socks, and I almost had a legit panic attack."

It's to Devon's absolute credit that he's listening to Nick and not staring at Ebony in her swimsuit as she sits on the edge of the pool.

"I think I'm channeling Holden Caulfield or something," Nick says. "Like proper existentialist angst and stuff. And a while ago I had all these feelings about dandelions that I'm pretty sure was exactly the same as watching my little sister on a carousel or whatever."

Devon lifts his hand to wipe his dripping hair back. "Do you want me to take you to a carousel so we can ride it?"

"No. The whole point is we don't get to ride the carousel anymore. We only get to watch the kids do it!"

"I don't think that's actually the point," Devon says, but he doesn't sound sure. "We can ride as many carousels as we want."

"But it's not the *same*," Nick tells him urgently. "Nothing's ever going to be the same."

Devon looks worried. "I know that, but we can't stop things from changing."

And that's the crux of it right there, Nick knows. It's exactly what he's so afraid of.

Whatever Devon is going to say next—and Nick likes to imagine that it would have been wise, thoughtful, and life-changing—is interrupted when, at the shallow end, Ebony pulls a screaming Shelley into the water.

"Should I get a tattoo?" Nick asks Devon later that night.

Devon snorts awake. "What?"

"A tattoo," Nick says, watching the sweep of light across his ceiling as a car drives down the street. "Shelley's only sixteen and she already has a tattoo."

"What would you get though?" Devon asks.

Nick thinks about it for a while. He likes the idea of a tattoo. He likes the idea of permanence, of picking something that's meaningful to him and wearing it on his skin forever. Except he's worried that he doesn't have anything that meaningful in his life. Would it be weird to get Devon's name? Yeah, probably. And while Nick has an incredibly long list of things he loves—Lord of the Rings, Star Wars, Harry Potter, and the Avengers, to name a few—he's not sure he wants to have anything from those franchises inked on his skin. He wants something that's his alone, maybe? He just doesn't know what that is.

"I wonder if Jai has any tattoos."

"You don't know?"

Nick shrugs and tugs the comforter over himself properly. "I haven't actually seen him naked yet."

"Dude, really?"

"Is that weird?"

"I don't know," Devon says. "Kind of? I mean, aren't you supposed to get naked with a fuck buddy?"

"I've seen his dick though. Just nothing else."

"I guess that's a start."

"It's a really nice dick," Nick tells him with a sigh.

"Good for you, bro," Devon says staunchly. For a straight guy, Devon is incredibly supportive. It's only fair, Nick figures, since he has to listen to Devon wax lyrical about girl parts. Which are cool and all, just absolutely not Nick's thing. But Nick is also supportive. Once, when Devon was dating a girl back in high school, Nick had even helped him research how to give oral. Seriously, the internet knows everything. Except how to alleviate a cramped tongue, apparently, which had been Devon's downfall in the end.

Nick sighs again and rolls over onto his side. He rests his head on Devon's chest, and Devon curls an arm around him. And it's probably a total violation of their cuddle bro code that Nick immediately wonders how it would feel to curl up with Jai like this.

"Are you thinking about Ebony right now?" he asks.

"Some part of me at least is always thinking about Ebony," Devon admits. "Does that make me a creepy stalker?"

"Um, are you actually stalking her?"

"No!"

"Then, no, you are not a creepy stalker."

"It's cool that we're friends and everything, and I think that maybe she'd be okay being more than friends, but what if I ask her and mess everything up?"

Nick thinks about it for a moment. "But what if you ask her and everything turns out great?"

"Seems like a big gamble," Devon says quietly.

"Relationships are hard," Nick murmurs.

"Yeah." Devon shakes his head. "You think we'll ever figure this stuff out?"

"Going on our track record, probably not."

"Probably not," Devon echoes, sounding pretty bummed. "Maybe we'll never figure anything out."

Nick's angst is either really contagious, or everyone has at least a bit of it. The thought is not as comforting as he'd like.

On Sunday night Nick is woken up by music. It's being played softly. He climbs out of bed and slips silently down the stairs. The lights are on in the living room. Nick peeks around the corner.

The coffee table has been moved.

Scooter the dog is sitting beside it, tail thumping noiselessly on the carpet.

Nick's jaw drops.

His mom and dad are *dancing*. Arms around each other, doing a slow sort of shuffle that Nick thinks means they don't know any actual dance steps. His mom is resting her head on his dad's shoulder. There's a gentle smile on her face, and her eyes are closed. His dad is nodding his head slightly, like he's trying to pay attention to the beat.

It may be the strangest thing Nick has ever seen. And he's seen every David Lynch movie ever made.

Is this what people do? Randomly dance together in the middle of the night? Or has Nick accidentally walked into some sort of otherworld where it turns out his parents are totally different people than he always thought? Except instead of having creepy buttons for eyes or something, they're *dancing*.

Nick feels suddenly overwhelmed, and he's not sure why. He can't even tease the threads of his conflicting emotions apart to trace them back to their source. It's sad, and it's beautiful, and everything and nothing all at the same time. It's a tiny flash of something bright that's buried too deep in ordinariness to ever shine.

His mom curls her hand around the back of his dad's neck, and her smile grows.

His parents are in *love*.

The sudden, acute awareness of it makes his throat ache and his eyes prick with tears.

A part of him wants to stay and watch, but he also doesn't want to see the dance end. He doesn't want to see them step apart and back into their mundane lives again. He heads upstairs, careful of the third step that always creaks, and slumps back down on his bed.

Under everything, twisted up with all those other threads into a complicated knot, Nick thinks he can draw out a string he recognizes: jealousy.

It would be nice, he thinks, to have someone to dance with in the night.

Nick: *What's your favorite place in the world?*
Jai: *1770, Australia.*
Nick: *That's a number.*
Jai: *It's a town.*

Some conversations can't be had via text. Nick calls Jai.

"What's so special about this place that I'm pretty sure you made up?"

"It's past midnight, Nick."

From downstairs, Nick can still hear the faint strains of music. "It's important?"

Jai sighs or yawns or something. "There's nothing really special about it, I guess. But I was stuck there for two days when I ran out of cash, and I just walked around and sat on the beach, and this old couple in an RV fed me and let me sleep in their camper when it rained."

"So it's not the place, it's the people?"

"Yeah."

Nick frowns at his ceiling. "Why do you have to go all the way around the world to meet nice people? There are nice people here."

"It's . . ." Jai hesitates. "It's not about people being nice. It's about going to somewhere totally different, and discovering that people are still people, you know?"

Nick's not sure he does.

"It's about realizing that the world is so much bigger than you ever knew, but also so much smaller."

"Oh." Wow. Jai really is Zen or something.

Jai sighs again. "Any more burning questions?"

"Do you have any tattoos?"

For a moment there's only silence, and Nick wonders if Jai ended the call. Then Jai huffs out a laugh. "That's for me to know and you to find out, isn't it?"

Nick squirms at the thought of it. "Challenge accepted!"

"Good night, Nick."

"Good night."
Nick drifts off with his phone still clutched in his hand.

CHAPTER  EIGHT

Nick: *I googled 1770. It is an actual town.*
Jai: *Yes, I know.*
Nick: *It just sounds really dumb.*
Jai: *Ok, but I didn't name it.*
Nick: *Fair point.*

Jai manages to pick up a few days' work with Bill Hollister. Bill lives down the street and runs a lawn mowing service. He usually has a guy help him out, but the guy's down with the chicken pox.

"The goddamn chicken pox," Bill grouses. "Who the hell gets the goddamn chicken pox?"

Jai just nods.

It takes a while for Bill to start his old truck, and then they're rattling their way over to the north side of town, where their first stop is a two-story brick place on half an acre. Bill gets the ride-on mower, while Jai gets to do all the legwork with the string trimmer.

"Still got that motorcycle, do ya?" Bill asks as he levers himself onto the mower.

"Yeah," Jai says.

Bill pats his left leg, which ends in a stump where his knee should be. "A 1973 Yamaha TX. I loved that fucking bike. Loved my leg too."

He starts the mower before Jai can think how to respond.

It's hot, hard work, and Jai feels like he's soaked in sweat within minutes. It's a lot like the construction site in that respect, but at least he's not covered in dust as well. Just grass clippings that stick to his legs. It takes less than an hour to finish the first yard, and then they load up the mower and hit the road again.

Bill likes to travel with the windows down, blasting Led Zeppelin and driving like a maniac. He'd be a hazard to other road users if the truck could actually get past thirty.

Throughout the day, whenever he gets a break, Jai finds himself checking his phone. He's oddly disappointed when he hasn't gotten any random texts from Nick.

This thing with Nick is . . . confusing. *Nick* is confusing. Or confounding. Probably both. But in one sense, while it's a no-strings arrangement, Jai has no idea how to navigate that with nine weeks still stretching out in front of them. Is he supposed to send Nick texts to see how his day is going? Or is he only supposed to text him to sort out a time to hook up? And of course Nick has no idea either, because Nick is eighteen and has never done this before. Jai doesn't know if Nick's even fooled around with anyone before him. Jai only knows Nick had never given head until that morning on the site, never gotten it until the other night, and unless he's done everything backward—Jai wouldn't be surprised, actually—he's still a virgin.

What's Jai supposed to do with that information anyway?

He doesn't want to push Nick, but he also doesn't want to treat him like he's made of glass. It's not up to Jai to be worried about if they're going too slow or too fast, is it? They're not dating. Except even though Nick's still practically a stranger, Jai does want them to part as friends. So it's something they have to talk about. How far does Nick want to take this, and what pace does he want to set?

Jesus. Hooking up is supposed to be easier than this.

"You got something troubling you, kid?" Bill demands when they're unloading the mower at the third house of the day.

"Not really," Jai lies.

"Damn straight," Bill says with a glower. "You're young, you're not too ugly, and you've still got both your fucking legs."

"That's a hell of a pep talk, Bill," Jai says, reaching up into the back of the truck for the string trimmer.

"I aim to please, kid." Bill grins broadly, showing his crooked teeth. "Now get the hell to work."

When they break for lunch, they buy sandwiches from a place in town that Bill swears by, then go and park behind an old warehouse to eat. At first Jai wonders why they're there, but then he notices the first cat. It's thin and wiry, with half an ear missing, but it approaches the parked truck fearlessly and leaps onto the hood. It stares at them through the cracked windshield and opens its mouth in a silent yowl.

"Impatient little prick," Bill says fondly, reaching around behind his seat to grab a small, battered cooler. He hauls it onto his lap and opens it, then tosses a slice of ham onto the cracked concrete of the parking lot. It lands with a faint slap, and the cat jumps down to retrieve it.

They're eventually joined by three more cats, and Bill tosses them the contents of the cooler, plus the crusts from his sandwich. Jai picks a few chunks of chicken out of his and drops them out the window. A calico cat darts forward to claim them.

"Right, then," Bill announces. "Back to work."

When he starts the truck again, the cats scatter.

The next day Jai brings some leftover meatloaf to feed the cats.

Jai: *The guy I'm mowing lawns with takes me to a warehouse every lunchtime and we feed stray cats.*
Nick: *That is AMAZING.*
Nick: *How many cats?*
Nick: *Do u pet them?*
Nick: *Do u have any pics?*
Nick: *I want a cat.*
Nick: *There is a shelter cat on Petfinder called Marigold is a Twinkly Magical Elf.*
Nick: *THAT'S ITS NAME!!!!!*
Nick: *I WANT IT!*
Nick: *Are u ALLOWED to call ur pets a whole phrase? This has opened up a new world for me.*
Nick: *Marigold is a Twinkly Magical Elf is in San Diego. :(*
Nick: *Why does the internet always crush my dreams like this?*
Jai: *I'm sorry for your loss. Are you good to hang out on Friday night?*
Nick: *Absolutely! :D*

Nick comes over again on Friday night, and this time Janice has opened the door and lured him into an awkward conversation before Jai can get to him. She's got a sleepy Noah hefted up on one hip, and Caden is peeking at Nick from behind the shelter of her legs.

"And what sort of job can you get with a criminology major?" Janice is asking when Jai reaches the top of the steps.

"Um." Nick grimaces a little. "Like profiling and stuff? Or some sort of law enforcement?"

Jai really can't imagine Nick as a cop. Going by the look on Nick's face, neither can he.

"Hey," he says. "Mom, Nick came over to hang out, not get grilled by you."

Janice waves it off. "We were just chatting, weren't we, Nick?"

"Yes?" he attempts hesitantly. The wide-eyed look he sends to Jai screams desperately for a rescue.

"Come on downstairs," Jai says, and Nick scuttles anxiously past Janice and the kids. He thumps down the steps to the basement and sags onto the couch.

Jai sits down next to him and opens his laptop.

"I've never met someone's mom before," Nick murmurs, and then starts. "I mean . . . No, I don't know what I mean. We're just hanging, right? Of course I've met my friends' moms before."

Jai smiles. He's not the only one struggling with fuck-buddy etiquette, then. "Well, I hope she didn't put you off too much."

"Nah."

"So, criminology?"

Nick looks a little haunted. "I didn't know what else to pick! My dad wanted me to do something with business, but that seemed like there might be a lot of math involved. And then it turns out there's, like, statistics and shit with criminology, so I'll probably just suck at that too."

"You don't like math?"

"Does anyone?" Nick asks darkly.

"I liked math in school."

"Ugh, of course you did." Nick rolls his eyes. "Because you have to be smart *and* hot." Then he winces. "Wow. Sometimes I just have no chill."

"Sometimes you barely speak English," Jai offers.

Nick grins and shrugs, then reaches out and tangles his fingers in Jai's. "True."

They're holding hands. Jai ignores the sudden spike of worry in him that, again, he doesn't know exactly how to define what they're doing here. It's nice. Why does he have to define it right now?

Nick rubs his thumb over Jai's palm, then lifts his hand so he can examine it. "You have blisters!"

"Yard work. I guess it hits a different spot than the calluses I got from construction."

"That's good." Nick wrinkles his nose. "Not the blisters, obviously, but the whole job thing."

"It was only a few days. I'm still looking for something that'll last the summer."

"Oh." Nick's face falls. "I'm really sorry for screwing up your job with Mr. Grover. Like, I get how much you love to travel and stuff."

"Not your fault. I told you that already." Jai shrugs. "Something will turn up."

Nick tilts his head. "Does it always?"

"Always," Jai tells him. "Anyway, if worst comes to worst, it's not like my mom will let me starve or anything."

Nick shows him a tentative smile, and drops his hand. "So, are you one of those guys who travels with a backpack the size of a postage stamp?"

"It's a little bigger than that," Jai says.

"How much bigger?"

Jai stands up and fetches his pack from the shelf above the washing machine. Just holding it makes him feel restless, like he needs to be on the move again. Always escaping, always chasing a new horizon. He runs his fingers over the scuffed nylon, then tugs at the straps.

"Seriously?" Nick asks. "I think my backpack for school was bigger than that! How do you fit in everything you need?"

"It's thirty liters." Jai sits back down on the couch and hands the pack over. "It's plenty big."

"What is this? A backpack for *ants*?" Nick demands, eyes wide and expectant, a smile tugging at his mouth.

"Okay, Zoolander," Jai says, pleased he caught the reference.

Nick laughs, delighted. "That's it! That's what we're watching tonight!"

Jai pulls the laptop closer and opens Netflix. "Good idea."

"Gonna . . ." Nick whispers in his ear, breath hot and fast. His fingers pluck at the hem of Jai's T-shirt. "Gonna search you for tattoos."

Jai hums in agreement, lifting his arms to let Nick pull the shirt off. The neckline snags under his jaw, suddenly gives, and Jai opens his eyes to see Nick tossing the shirt onto the floor. Then Nick's crowding him against the back of the couch, like he's trying to climb into his lap or—

Oh, okay. That's exactly what he's trying to do. Jai relaxes, and Nick straddles his thighs. Denim scrapes against denim. Jai puts his hands on Nick's hips, because this is *Nick*. He'll probably take a nosedive any second now and kill the mood. Nick arches his spine, and Jai tightens his grip just in case. Then Nick leans forward again, resting a hand on Jai's chest. He bites his lip as his fingers tremble slightly against Jai's skin.

"So, um, none here," he says, his cheeks pinking up.

"No, none there."

Nick makes a breathless sound that may be part laugh, then slides his shaking hand down Jai's chest. Jai's not sure he can remember the last time he was touched so tentatively. He laces his fingers through Nick's, pressing Nick's hand more firmly to his chest.

Nick drags his hand lower.

Jai hears a buzzing sound in his head.

No, not in his head, because Nick's suddenly leaning back and digging into the pocket of his jeans. He pulls his phone out and stares at the screen. "Oh crap."

Jai raises his eyebrows. "Problem?"

Nick sighs. "Just a text from my mom saying she and Dad got pizza tonight."

Jai frowns.

"Meaning," Nick says, "they went to Pizza Perfecto. Meaning they saw that Devon was at work, and clearly I am not at his house, because why would I be at his house when he's at work? Meaning I'm busted."

"Busted for what?"

"Well, I'm not grounded exactly," Nick says, then catches the look Jai gives him. "I am eighteen, I swear! It says so on my driver's license. It's just kind of a 'while you're living under my roof, you'll follow my rules, young man' situation. I mean, they've been pretty good about the whole getting-fired thing, but I didn't exactly tell them I was hanging out with you, or with anyone. Except Devon, in which case it really only would have been hanging out. I think they think that if they let me leave the house unaccompanied, I'll somehow throw myself headfirst into someone's creepy sex dungeon or something."

"As opposed to someone's creepy basement?"

Nick pokes him in the shoulder. "This is a *nice* basement. Anyway, long story short, I'm supposed to be proving I can behave, not—" he waves his hand "—this. Us. You."

Jai's confusion must be written all over his face.

Nick slides off Jai's lap and slumps on the couch beside him. He cards his fingers through his hair, leaving it standing up at odd angles. "They're still treating me like a kid, even though legally I'm not, but I can't really fault them, you know? I haven't really given them any other options. I mean, I still do feel like a kid, and most of the time I'm totally on board with that. Adulting is overrated."

"'Adulting' is not a word."

"Is too." Nick cracks a grin. "See? 'Is too.' I'm twelve years old."

Jai groans. "Please don't say that."

"Why?"

"Because it makes me feel like a creep."

Nick snorts. "Do you want to see my driver's license, dude? For real?"

"No," Jai says, but kind of does.

Nick sighs again. "Thinking about my parents has really killed the mood, hasn't it?" He doesn't wait for an answer. "I should probably go and face the music."

Jai looks at him. "Is this going to mess up hanging out?"

It's the first time he's noticed they've both started calling it that. Maybe because they both have no idea what else to call it.

"No way, dude." Nick climbs to his feet and straightens his rumpled shirt. "You are the most important part of my plan to get a dick inside me before college."

Well, so much for needing to have that conversation.

Nick sucks in a quick breath. "Um, I mean, if you're cool with that. Because, clear and explicit consent and all that. But, cards very much on the table here, I really would like you to have sex with me. Like, penetrative." He screws his face up. "Wow, that's an ugly word, isn't it? Penetrative."

"We could agree never to say it again," Jai suggests. "But if you're asking if I want that too, then yes. I'm also versatile."

"Yeah, I know. You like the dudes *and* the ladies."

"Yeah," Jai says slowly, waiting for the penny to drop. It doesn't. "But I mean that if you wanted to fuck me too, I'd say yes."

Nick's eyes widen. He opens and shuts his mouth a few times before words come out. "Seriously?"

Jai leans down to pluck his T-shirt from the floor. "Why wouldn't I be serious about that?"

Nick is silent for a long moment. Then he seems to shake himself awake. "I . . . I don't know." He gestures at himself, his hands jerking. "Because I'm me and you're *you*?"

"You think because you fit the description of a twink that you can't top?"

Nick narrows his eyes, like he suspects a trap. "Maybe?"

"You need to find more porn," Jai tells him.

"Lack of porn has never been a problem for me before. Trust me."

"Better porn, then. Porn where bigger, older guys are getting absolutely plowed by twinks. See if you like it."

Nick's eyes actually glaze over. "I," he begins, then stops. He draws a deep breath. "I will get right on that. Thanks, dude!"

Then, before Jai wonders if he should get up and kiss him good-bye, or hug him, or just shake his hand—although that would feel odd—Nick's clattering back up the stairs and disappearing.

CHAPTER  NINE

The empty Pizza Perfecto box sits open on the kitchen table, the bottom spotted with grease and crumbs, and adorned with a single stray slice of gray, shiny mushroom curled up like a little slug. Nick's stomach growls, but he heroically ignores it. He sits down at the table and pats the dog's head when she presses it insistently against his knee. He likes to imagine that she's being fiercely loyal and can sense his distress, but most likely she just thinks there's still pizza left.

"Where were you tonight?" his mom asks in a casual tone, but Nick knows there's nothing casual about this.

His dad is standing by the counter, arms crossed. His mom goes to stand beside him, and he leans into her a little, just like when they were dancing.

"I was at a friend's," Nick says.

"You said you were at Devon's," his mom reminds him.

Heat rises in Nick's face. "I was at another friend's. Like a *boyfriend's*."

If the word sounds like a lie, it's because it is. But Nick figures it's much better to lie about what Jai is to him than hit his parents with the truth: *Mom, Dad, I have a fuck buddy!*

His mom frowns. "You have a boyfriend?"

Nick nods.

"Why haven't you—" his mom begins.

"How old is he?" his dad cuts in, and whoa, Dad, way to go right for the jugular. Has Nick been wearing a flashing neon sign that says: *Fooling around with an unnecessarily hot twenty-five-year-old*? Really, seven years isn't that much of a difference, except when it comes to, well, everything. Like life experience, of which Nick has none. And he definitely isn't going to think about how, when Jai first picked up his ridiculously tiny backpack and headed off to see the world, Nick was still in middle school.

"Um, he's like around twenty, I think," Nick lies.

"Where did you meet?" his mom asks.

Nick's gaze falls on the pizza box. "At Pizza Perfecto. He's one of Dev's regulars."

"You're supposed to be getting work and thinking about college," his dad says, a hard edge to his voice.

"Yeah, Dad, I know," Nick says. "And I am. But I've hung out with him a few times. It's not like I'm there all the time or anything. I don't even see him every day. It's a couple of hours a week."

The truth should sound different than a lie, right? Nick's been weaving the two so tightly together for so long that he's not sure even he can tell the difference anymore. He wants to believe that most of his lies come from a good place. He doesn't want his parents to worry. But then he also doesn't want them to hassle him, so it's maybe not totally altruistic. Or at all.

"You lied to us," his dad says.

"Yeah." Nick tugs the dog's ears gently. "I'm sorry."

His dad sighs. When Nick can finally bring himself to look up, his dad has left the kitchen.

His mom sits down across from him. "Are you being safe, Nick?"

Nick flushes. "Yes, Mom."

"Like with condoms?" she clarifies, horribly.

"Yes!" Well, not exactly, but they've only given each other head, right? Which is almost safe, right? And it's not like Nick has anything. Jai, though, has probably fucked his way around the world two or three times. Who wouldn't, if they looked like that? "I'm being safe, Mom."

She shows him a hesitant smile. "And maybe you could invite your friend over for dinner one night?"

"Um, we're not . . ." Nick shrugs. "It's kind of new and casual, you know?"

Her face falls a little.

"I'll ask him though," Nick offers. It may be another lie. He isn't sure. "Would Dad be cool with that?"

"Of course he would," his mom says.

Something about her tone rings false to Nick. His mom's not as good a liar as he is. But he smiles anyway, and pretends he believes it.

Devon: *I asked Ebony out! We're going to a movie on Wednesday night. Holy fuck!*

Nick: *Proud of u, bro.*

Devon: *Don't let me mess this up, k?*

Nick: *You won't! {}*

Devon: *What is that?*

Nick: *It's a hug. I'm hugging u, Devon.*

Devon: *I'm so psyched. But also terrified. This is EBONY! EBONY!*

Nick: *You'll do fine, Dev. You're cute, and you're tall, and you have nice hair.*

Devon: *???*

Nick: *You are also smart and wonderful and give the best hugs. If u were gay, I would have jumped u years ago.*

Devon: *U sort of did.*

Nick: *And u were very cool about it, my poor confused little straight boy.*

Devon: *Because of u I thought I was gay for a week.*

Nick: *You're welcome!*

Devon: *Also, Marlene quit today. Pauly says u can have her job as long as u don't blow anyone on staff in work time.*

Nick: *SERIOUSLY? You want me to work with u? Aw babe, did u miss me?*

Devon: *U complete me.*

Nick: *Awww. ILY.*

Devon: *ILY too, bro.*

Nick floats in the pool, eyes closed. It's dark, and the breeze is a little cool, but it's too nice to move. If he goes inside, he'll have to peel off his wet board shorts, and remember to hang his towel up, and have a shower, and then find another towel, and that all seems like too much hard work when it's so peaceful just floating here, tiny waves lapping at his skin.

When he was a kid, Nick used to like floating facedown and watching the way his hair spread out around him in the water like a dancing anemone. Until one day, screaming, his mom launched herself fully clothed into the pool, thinking he'd drowned. So after that he wasn't allowed to "play tricks" in the pool. It had seemed easier to admit he'd been pranking her than to try to explain what he'd been doing, when Nick wasn't sure himself.

He also used to tie his legs together and pretend he was a mermaid.

No, wait.

Mer*man*. He was a merman, damn it.

That progressed to tying his wrists together too, and pretending he was an escape artist who was fast running out of air. After coming too close for comfort one day, he'd sworn to himself never to try that again. He still remembers the sick thrill of thinking he was actually going to die. How afterward he felt so alive that every color in the world seemed brighter for it.

He's not an adrenaline junkie though.

He doesn't even like roller coasters.

What he likes is . . .

What he likes is the thrill of kissing Jai Hazenbrook, and blowing him and being blown, and coming under his touch. He likes kissing him and feeling a shiver. He likes the way Jai's touch lights him up at every point and makes electricity arc through him like he's one of those plasma globes. Nick doesn't need near-death experiences or roller coasters. Nick knows exactly where to get all his thrills. Tonight they didn't even do much, and it was still amazing.

Nick pulls his fingers through the water, testing the drag.

He likes Jai in a new, quiet way that has nothing to do with how hot Jai is, but also doesn't take anything away from that. Because how could it? Jai is incredible. He's hot, but he's also hotter than that because he's not a dick about it. And he must know, right? His house must have mirrors. Failing that, he's got to notice the way that people do cartoonish double-takes when they see him, jaws dropping, eyes bulging, hearts and twittering birds magically appearing. But he's still not a dick about it.

Nick opens his eyes and stares up at the stars.

If Nick were that hot, he'd be a dick about it. An arrogant, smarmy dick who got laid every night. He'd wear a shirt that said, *Don't hate me because I'm beautiful*, and people would think it was ironic, but it secretly wouldn't be. He'd probably end up with a reality TV show of his own, because the only reason that people always say, "It doesn't matter what you look like, it only matters who you are *inside*," is because they feel the need to say it every time life proves them wrong, and it happens a lot.

Devon's been saying it to Nick for ages.

There was a kid in junior year who Nick crushed on pretty badly. His name was Ash, and he was cute and cool and also gay. And when Nick finally worked up the courage to approach him—not even to ask him out, since he never got that far—Ash just put a hand on his chest and shook his head: *"Nuh-uh, short stuff."*

It still stings to remember it. Nick had spent ages thinking about the things that Ash might like, and the things they could talk about, and the movies and music they probably had in common, but Ash didn't care about any of that stuff, all because Nick wasn't tall enough.

"He's just a dick," Devon said staunchly. *"If he doesn't want to get to know you, that's his loss, bro, not yours."*

Except how was it Ash's loss? He'd find some taller boy who fitted him just fine, and he'd be happy, and it would never even occur to him that maybe he should have taken a chance on the short kid.

"It doesn't matter that you're short," Devon said. *"You're a good guy."*

Sure. A good guy who would literally be overlooked every time.

Jai doesn't care that Nick is short. Okay, so maybe that's because Nick offered to suck his dick that day on the site. That's an icebreaker, probably. But also Jai doesn't care because Jai is definitely not shallow. He is the opposite of shallow. He has *depth*. He has a tiny backpack for ants and he doesn't care about material possessions and he travels the world.

He also offered to let Nick fuck him.

Holy *shit*.

The memory of that conversation hits him in the guts like a sledgehammer.

Welp. Nick can either lie in the pool all night, getting colder by the hour, or he can head upstairs with that thought in his head, and jerk off furiously until he collapses.

Nick goes with option two.

Jai: *Did your parents get angry?*
Nick: *It's cool. Ish.*
Jai: *Good.*
Nick: *Turns out there's a whole world of porn out there with twinks fucking older guys.*
Jai: *Told you.*
Nick: *It's hot.*
Jai: *You're interested?*
Nick: *Very much so!*
Nick: *BTW, do u like making pizza?*
Jai: *I guess.*
Nick: *Like at a ship.*
Nick: **shop*
Nick: *Pizza Perfecto is hiring. My friend Devon works there. Can probably get u the job if you're interested.*
Jai: *Yeah, that would be great.*
Nick: *I'll get Dev to text u with the details if u want.*
Jai: *Thanks.*
Nick: *K. Good night.*
Jai: *Good night.*

On Monday, Nick takes his dad lunch at his office. It was his mom's suggestion when, racing out the front door ten minutes after Chris, she noticed he'd forgotten his lunch. So at 11 a.m., hoping that's not too late—what time does his dad eat lunch, anyway?—Nick heads downtown with his dad's lunch slung in a plastic grocery bag over the handlebars of his bike.

He's really starting to hate his bike.

When he gets to his dad's office, he considers leaving his bike outside in the hope it gets stolen, but in the end wheels it into reception with an apologetic smile for Charlene, the firm's receptionist.

"Nicky!" she exclaims, like he's still five years old. "How are you, sweetheart?"

"Good," Nick says. "Um, sorry about my bike."

She waves his concerns away. "Just lean it up against the wall there. I'll buzz you through."

Chris Stahlnecker is an accountant. He's a partner in the firm, which is not as exciting as it sounds. It's not like he works on the top floor of some glass-and-steel monolith in New York or something. He works in a two-story brick building in downtown Franklin, and brings his lunch from home. A sandwich and an apple and a tiny container of potato salad. Talk about the high life.

Treading his way upstairs, Nick wonders if his dad ever just wants to scream and go all Michael Douglas in *Falling Down*. He wonders if his dad is happy with life and with the way the regimented days stretch out in front of him, every one like the one before, and then he wonders if he could ever just ask him a question as naked as that.

His dad is on the phone when Nick reaches his office. He frowns questioningly, and Nick holds the bag up. His dad points at his desk, and Nick shuffles inside and sets his lunch down. Then, because it would probably be rude to walk away without even saying hello, he sits down across from his dad.

His dad ends his call. "Nick. Mom said you were bringing my lunch. Thanks."

Is it weird that his dad calls his mom "Mom"? That seems weird, but then most people's parents do it, right? But once upon a time his parents were Chris and Marnie, and then Nick turned up and they reframed themselves. They shifted their perspectives to align with Nick's, and that seems like a really strange thing. He wonders, when he goes to college, if they'll have to relearn their own names.

"It's no problem," he says, and waits for his dad to point out that of course it's not, since Nick doesn't have a job to go to. Then he thinks about Friday night, and how his dad left the kitchen when Nick said he'd been with a guy. "Does it bother you I have a boyfriend?"

His dad meets his gaze. "It bothers me that you lie."

It would be easier, probably, if his dad just didn't like the fact he was gay. It would give Nick something to rail against, because he can't help being gay. But he makes a choice to lie, every single time. "I'm sorry."

His dad drags the grocery bag across his desk and unpacks his lunch. His sandwich. His apple. His little container of potato salad. He lines them up in a row, then scrunches the grocery bag up and drops it in his trash can. "Did you want anything else, Nick?"

Nick kind of wants to listen to Fall Out Boy at top volume and yell and punch a few walls, actually, but he only shakes his head and stands up again. "See you later, Dad."

"Good-bye, Nick."

When he gets back to the lobby and collects his bike, he discovers the grips of the handlebars have left black smudges against the otherwise pristine wall.

CHAPTER  TEN

On Wednesday morning, Jai turns up at Pizza Perfecto and meets the owner, Pauly. Fifteen minutes after that, he's being shown his locker and given a T-shirt that promises Pizza Perfecto is Franklin's best pizza parlor.

"Okay, so we'll start you off on the day shift," Pauly says. He's in his mid-to-late thirties, Jai guesses. Pudgy around the middle, probably because he owns a pizza parlor, with dark hair that's beginning to thin on his crown. "It can get a little busy, but it's nothing like evenings. Tips are shared with the team you're on shift with. You okay with that?"

"Yeah."

"It's mostly part-timers here," Pauly says. "We'll start you on a trial for the first week, then if you want longer hours, we can fit you in. Now Marlene's gone, I could use someone to open in the mornings. Most of these kids are still in bed at 10 a.m."

"I worked construction," Jai tells him. "Ten a.m. is not going to be a problem."

Pauly gives him a quick run-through of how to work the register, and that's it. He's then officially a part of the team. Jai works his first shift that day, wishing he'd at least had a chance to wash his T-shirt first. It's new and itchy. But the work is easy enough, even though some orders are a little out there. Who orders pizza without cheese? At least three people in that first lunchtime shift, so it's obviously not as uncommon as Jai would have thought.

Jai has his second shift on Thursday evening, and, yeah, it's much busier. The delivery guys don't even have time to sit in the alley out back and chat, and the crew in the kitchen works to a rhythm Jai can only admire from a safe distance, moving seamlessly around one another in the relatively tight space.

The team working the evening is mostly a younger crowd.

"Hey, Jai, right?" A tall kid with scruffy blond hair and gray eyes introduces himself. "I'm Devon, Nick's friend."

Jai shakes his hand. "Nice to meet you. And thanks for getting me the job."

Devon shrugs. "Nick said you needed it, so."

So? But Devon doesn't elaborate.

Working with a bunch of high schoolers and recent high school graduates is both fun and frustrating. Is Jai seriously the only one with enough initiative to run the mop over the floor or refill the napkin dispensers when there's a lull? Because that's apparently when the rest of the crew kicks back, turns the music up, and plays indoor baseball with a breadstick and olives.

When Jai asks what they'll say if Pauly turns up and catches them, Devon just laughs. "Dude, Pauly taught us this!"

Jai watches as Casey pitches an olive to Ebony. She swings the breadstick, hits it, and the olive ricochets off the cheap print of the Colosseum on the back wall.

"Woot!" Devon throws his arms up. "She hits it out of the ballpark!"

"You guys are idiots," Jai tells them with a grin.

This is going to be the easiest job Jai's ever had.

"You smell like cheese," Caden says when Jai gets home from work after his lunchtime shift on Friday. His face lights up when Jai sets the pizza box down on the coffee table in the living room. "Pizza! Yay!"

He drops his video game controller and dives in.

Jai grins at his enthusiasm.

It's good having a job again. Jai didn't realize how much pressure he'd been feeling until it was gone. Suddenly the future is looking a lot brighter. The money from the pizza parlor isn't anywhere close to what he was earning in construction, but Jai can make it work. He can go online and browse pictures of Argentina without his stomach clenching up with the possibility of failure.

It also takes some pressure off his mom, because an unemployed Jai isn't just a Jai who'll be stuck living in the basement, it's a Jai who'll also need feeding. And things are a little too tight for that not to be an issue. Janice would hardly let him starve, but Jai's noticed how most of the brand-name products in the kitchen have slowly been switched out with generic substitutes. It's only little things like that and the faulty hot-water system, but they all add up. Having work means taking the pressure off the family as well.

Jai sits on the sagging armchair across from the couch. He glances over at Kat. Her hair is bright purple and cut into a jagged, asymmetrical bob. "What the hell happened to you?"

Kat checks Caden isn't watching before she shows Jai her middle finger.

Jai leans forward and snags a piece of pizza. "Looks good."

"Ronny said I look like a clown."

"Well, Ronny has a face like a butt," Jai offers.

From somewhere in the house, he hears Ronny laugh.

"Jesus, am I the only person who went to work today?"

"Oh, how the tables have turned, right?" Kat asks. "I'm on my half day, and Ronny had another interview this morning, so hopefully that will work out."

"What about you, Caden?"

"Vacation," Caden tells him through a mouthful of pizza.

Ronny wanders in, Noah on his hip. Kat makes room for him on the couch, and he sits. Noah wriggles to reach the pizza, so Ronny takes a slice and picks off a few pieces of olive for him to try.

"You had an interview?" Jai asks.

"Yeah, for a permanent spot over at the high school in Lebanon."

"Good luck," Jai says.

"Yeah." Ronny sighs. "I could use some of that. I'm sick of subbing, and I hate summer school already."

Jai sees the way that Kat links her fingers with Ronny's and squeezes.

Caden squirms into a space he makes between Ronny's knees. "Daddy? Want to play *Mario Kart* with me?"

Ronny runs his free hand through Caden's hair. "After pizza, okay?"

"Okay." Caden leans into him.

"How about we give Uncle Jai a turn as well?" Ronny asks.

Jai snorts. "Last time I played *Mario Kart*, it was on an N64."

"Good," Ronny says. "I might actually beat you, then."

"Bring it," Jai says, and Caden crows and claps and gets so excited he drops his pizza on the carpet.

On Saturday night Jai looks up to greet his next customer, and discovers that it's Nick. He's wearing a faded T-shirt and skinny jeans.

"Hey."

"Hey." Nick jams his hands in his pockets and looks around. "Pretty busy, huh?"

"Yeah, it has been. I think the family in the booth at the back is just finishing up if you want a seat."

"I usually hang out in the kitchen if it's full," Nick tells him. "Pauly doesn't care."

Yeah, Jai is pretty sure that's Pauly's life motto.

Over at the last booth, the mom is levering her kid out of a spaghetti-splattered high chair, and the dad is signing off on the bill. Ebony is already there with a smile, helping the mom untangle the kid's ankle from one of the straps. Then, the moment they're gone, she's wiping down the table and gesturing for Nick.

"Guess you got a spot," Jai says.

"Guess I did." Nick grins.

It's almost eight, which means the dinner crowd is leaving and the drunk crowd won't be turning up for a few more hours. Most of them don't sit in the booths anyway. They usually buy their pizza by the slice and then stagger off down the street with it. They tip incredibly well too. Crumpled notes and handfuls of coins they're too wasted to figure out. Often the entire contents of pockets ends up in the tip jar: condoms, phone numbers, keys, and, last night, a cell phone.

"What's he ordering?" Jai asks when Ebony fetches Nick a Coke from behind the counter.

"Nick always gets the staff special," Ebony says.

The staff special. The kitchen crew makes up a few per shift. It's whatever pizza they feel like eating, but "ruined" with the wrong sort of cheese, or slightly burned around the edges, or some other thing that makes it unfit to sell to the public. It's another thing Pauly absolutely doesn't care about.

"Nick's not staff," Jai says.

Ice clinks as Ebony shoves the glass against the dispenser. She raises her eyebrows. "He *would* have been."

Jai's distracted by a woman rushing inside to collect a phone order. By the time he turns back, Ebony's gone, and over in his booth, Nick is jabbing a clump of ice with his straw and reading something on his phone.

Devon moves in behind the counter to get someone's bill.

"Devon?"

"Mmm?" Devon is poking at the register and squinting at the screen like he's not sure he can believe whatever it's telling him. Apparently he likes math just as much as Nick.

"Did Nick apply for the job here too?"

"No." Devon glances up and shrugs. "I asked him if he wanted it, and he said Pauly should hire you instead. He'll probably be stuck riding his bike all summer."

"Why?"

"His dad won't let him get his car back until he gets a job. Because of the whole—" Devon makes a vague gesture "—*thing*." He catches Jai's blank look. "The whole blowjob thing?"

Jai clears his throat. "Right."

Devon takes the bill over to the waiting customers, and Jai watches Nick out of the corner of his eye as he works. He feels a rush of affection for Nick. Recommending him for the job was a nice gesture. It may even be more than that. Jai doesn't know if Nick really wanted the job or not. Maybe he's happier doing nothing and having to ride his bike instead of drive his car, but, even so, it's still a nice gesture. It's generous. He didn't just turn down a job. He remembered how much Jai needed one.

When Jai gets his break, he heads into the kitchen to grab a few slices of the staff special, loads them onto a plate, and joins Nick in the booth.

"Hey."

Nick sets his phone aside and grins. "Hey."

Jai slides the pizza toward him.

"Dude, I just ate two slices," Nick says, but takes another one anyway. "What time are you working until tonight?"

"I finish at ten."

"That's excellent. So, like, are you kind of free after that?"

"Nah." Jai gives Nick a second to look disappointed. "Got a hot date. With you."

Nick makes a sound caught somewhere between a snort and a giggle, and then widens his eyes in mortification. "Oh, wow. I'm so smooth."

You're cute, Jai wants to tell him, but just laughs instead. "You keep telling yourself that."

They eat their pizza.

Nick: *STOP LOOKING AT ME!*
Devon: *Dude, I'm not even.*
Nick: *U r. It's making me nervous.*
Devon: *He's totally into u.*
Nick: *STOP TEXTING ME!*
Devon: *Show him some nip, bro.*

Nick flails, squawks, and almost knocks over his soda in his haste to shove his phone back in his pocket.

Jai reaches out and steadies Nick's wobbling glass. "Okay?"

Nick shoots a narrow look at the counter, where for some reason Devon is grinning like a lunatic. "Um, yep!"

"Devon says you don't have your car."

Nick nods. "I rode my bike."

"I'll give you a ride to my place when my shift's over," Jai offers.

Nick's jaw drops. "On your motorbike?"

"Is that a problem?"

Nick grins. "It is the opposite of a problem! Except I've never been on one before, so is there anything I need to know?"

"You just hold on," he says, warming at the idea of Nick's arm around him. "Let me take care of the rest."

Jai doesn't even realize how filthy that may sound until Nick's eyes widen and then glaze over, and he starts rubbing his straw against his bottom lip in an incredibly distracting way.

"Nick?"

Nick starts. "Yeah, yeah, that sounds good! I'll get Devon to take my bike home in his truck." He glares at his phone. "He owes me."

Jai looks over to Devon, who suddenly grabs the cordless phone by the cash register and starts taking someone's order loudly, even though Jai would swear the phone hasn't rung. When it suddenly does, Devon drops it in surprise, and then doubles over laughing.

"You guys are idiots," Jai tells Nick with a smile.

Nick is laughing too, so hard that he's bright red, and all he can do is laugh louder and nod in response.

CHAPTER  ELEVEN

This may be the greatest moment of Nick's life. Apart from the time he sucked Jai's dick, maybe. And vice versa. But in terms of things Nick feels comfortable sharing on social media afterward, this is obviously the greatest moment of his life.

"You good?" Jai asks, adjusting the straps on the motorbike helmet, and okay, great, now Nick feels about five years old.

"Yeah, let's do this!"

Jai straddles his bike.

It's hot. His jeans pull tight against his ass, and the tendons in his forearms cord as he grips the handlebars, and . . .

Wait. Are they still called handlebars on a motorbike? Nick actually knows nothing about motorbikes, except that he's about to ride one, like, pressed up against Jai. With his arms around him and everything. And there will be a throbbing engine that will, well, *throb*. It's going to be fucking incredible.

"Come on, then," Jai says with a grin.

"Am I wearing a helmet because you think I'm going to fall off?" Nick asks, eyeing the bike and trying to figure out how to climb on.

"You're wearing the helmet because I only brought one," Jai tells him, which may just be a way of avoiding giving a straight answer. "Now get up here."

"Oh Jesus," Nick says under his breath, and clambers on. Is he supposed to stand on that thing? That's a foot peg, right, not something mechanically critical? But at last he manages to swing a leg over the bike and get his ass on the seat. He lands heavily, and the slope of the seat immediately means he's slipping forward and shoving his dick against Jai's ass. His already hard dick. Nick thinks it's been hard since Jai offered to take him for a ride on his bike.

Fuck.

Who is he kidding? It's been hard since the moment he set eyes on Jai Hazenbrook and his incredible ass that day weeks ago in Mr. Grover's office. Years from now, when Nick tells the story of his summer romance, he's going to say he noticed Jai's eyes first. That will be a lie. Nick is pretty sure he didn't notice Jai even had eyes. Because, really? That *ass*. It draws attention away from everything else Jai has going for him. Which is *literally* everything else. Jai is perfection in a way that shouldn't be allowed to live outside Middle Earth or the Marvel universe. He probably doesn't even have a single toenail that grows in a weird, gnarled way.

"Hold on," Jai says.

Nick slides his arms around Jai's waist.

Jai starts the bike.

Oh God. It's like leaning against the washing machine when it's on the spin cycle but way, *way* more intense. It's very possible that Nick has died and gone to heaven. The vibrations of the engine are thrumming through him, and settling right in his *balls*, and do motorcycle manufacturers know what a public safety hazard these things must be? How is anyone supposed to keep an eye on the road when all they can think about is their balls? Clearly this is why they're so dangerous.

When Jai hits the throttle, Nick meeps.

Like Beaker from the Muppets.

Luckily the engine is so loud that Jai probably doesn't notice. And he doesn't seem to mind when Nick tightens his arms convulsively and clings to him like a slightly terrified possum.

Nick squeezes his eyes shut for a moment, and when he opens them again, the bike is moving. The storefronts zip past in a blur that seems so much more terrifying and exhilarating than when Nick watches from behind a windshield. It's probably the way that Nick can feel the wind tugging at him. Or maybe because of the way he can feel Jai's muscles shifting under his hands whenever he moves. Yeah, it's probably the second thing.

It would be a really, really bad idea to slide one hand down Jai's jeans, right?

Yes. Yes, it would.

Nick keeps his hands where they are. Regretfully.

It takes Nick a few minutes to get used to the bike, and then everything he thinks he's learned goes flying out the nonexistent window when they take a corner, and Nick sees exactly how fucking close the road is to his head. His stomach does the flippity-floppity thing it usually reserves for roller coasters, whenever Devon can bully him into going on one. It's much easier, though, to put his trust in Jai than it is to put his trust in some faceless and possibly incompetent cabal of roller-coaster engineers.

By the time they take their second corner, Nick's fear has transformed into a sort of breathless joy. This is *fun*. It's also superhot and sexy. And, when they pull up at a red light, Nick gets to preen a little when two middle-aged ladies in a hatchback look over at him and Jai enviously. Also lustfully. Because Jai is hot as fuck. That's, like, an objective scientific truth, the same as gravity. Nick doesn't know how either one works exactly, but they're both demonstrable facts.

And, behind his helmet, Nick could be hot as fuck too, for all those ladies know. It feels like Nick's probably not going to get a lot of chances to play out a fantasy like this one, so he's going to enjoy it, okay? He makes a show of running a hand over Jai's jean-clad thigh.

Okay, it's not *just* for the benefit of the ladies in the hatchback.

Jai turns his head, grinning, and says something that's lost to a roar of the engine as they speed off again, leaving the hatchback behind them. Nick very quickly puts his hand back where it was, and holds on.

This is so cool.

Nick is actually disappointed when they get to Jai's house and Jai stops the bike.

He climbs off, unfastens the helmet, and removes it. He's pretty sure it leaves his hair doing weird things, but who cares about that? He just rode on a motorbike!

"That was so great!" he exclaims, hugging the helmet because, no, he never wants to give it back, thanks very much. If he keeps it, Jai will have to keep taking him for rides, right? That's probably how it works.

Jai laughs and takes his hand and leads him inside the house.

It's late, and all the lights are off. Jai knows where he's going though, and Nick follows him and just hopes he won't knock into anything on the way. When they reach the door to the basement, Jai opens it and flicks the light on, and Nick follows him downstairs.

He sets the helmet down on the scuffed coffee table regretfully, and then lets out an embarrassing whimper when he turns around to find Jai tugging his shirt off. It's like . . . it's like there should be music playing in the background, and some sort of product placement. Maybe for aftershave. Or expensive razors. Or any other sort of commercial that Nick jerked off to furtively when he was twelve, before he discovered GayTube. Which was both a red-letter day *and* a day that will forever live in infamy. A happy, dirty, confusing, guilt-ridden hell of a day. What can Nick say? GayTube very much shaped the person he is today. He won't apologize for that.

"I stink of pizza," Jai says when he gets his shirt over his head. He balls it up and flings it into the corner closest to the washing machine.

"I like pizza," Nick says slowly, unable to tear his gaze away from Jai's abs. Wild horses couldn't even. Nick will stab them if they try.

Jai's grin turns a little predatory, and that is totally okay with Nick. Jai steps toward him. "Maybe you stink of pizza too, huh?"

"What? No, not really." Nick sniffs experimentally, and then catches Jai's questioning look and flushes. "Oh, okay, was that like some hint for me to take my shirt off as well?"

"It was."

"Oh, dude, no, you really need to spell shit out for me if you're going to be all like—" Nick waves his hand at Jai's ridiculous abs. "All like hot and in my face and whatnot. My blood isn't exactly running to my brain, yeah?"

Because abs. And also nipples.

Nick is already hard. Well, okay, he's been hard since he straddled Jai's motorbike, but that's splitting hairs. Nick had thought that once he was getting off regularly with someone other than his own hand, he'd maybe learn some control or something? Get just enough experience to say, *Hey there, boner, what do you say you settle the fuck down for a minute, huh?* That does not appear to have happened at all. Nick probably needs *more* experience.

Jai's smile and his laugh are just perfect, and how is he even a little bit real?

More to the point, why does he want to fool around with Nick when clearly he could have any man or woman on the planet?

Look, Nick hasn't got terrible self-esteem or anything, but he is a realist. He has eyes. He knows he's not a troll, exactly. In a favorable light he could possibly be the mild-mannered librarian alter ego of a superhero. But Jai? Jai is like winning the sexual lottery, if there were such a thing.

Note to self: pitch that as a reality TV show. For now, remove shirt.

Nick tugs his Alderaan Fire Department T-shirt over his head, drops it on the floor, and steps forward into Jai's space because now it's time to man the fuck up. He puts one hand on Jai's shoulder and tilts his jaw for a kiss.

Jai Hazenbrook is the only guy Nick has ever kissed. He kissed a girl once, but that probably doesn't count because it was for spin the bottle, and also he was too drunk to actually remember it happening. He only saw it on Facebook the next day. But even though he's not really experienced, Nick is pretty sure they're doing this right. It feels too good to be wrong. Jai takes the lead, because he knows what the hell he's doing, but it's not long before Nick is kissing him back and easing his tongue into Jai's mouth.

Strange what a tiny bit of contact can do. Two wet muscles sliding against one another—and okay, that sounds gross—but it's somehow electric. It makes Nick shiver. Makes him feel flushed. Makes his erection twitch and his balls ache.

Making out is awesome, but it's also a huge tease, because the need for more twists tighter and tighter in Nick until he's gripping Jai's shoulders roughly and trying to climb him like a tree. He's got one leg hooked around Jai's thigh when Jai finally takes pity on him and gets his hands under Nick's ass and lifts him. Then, instead of to the couch where Nick figured they were headed, he lugs Nick over to the wall, props him up against it, and gets a thigh between his legs. Nick straddles him like he straddled the bike. And, yes, things are throbbing again.

Jai leans away a little, breaking the kiss. His gaze rakes over Nick, and then he pushes forward and licks a stripe along Nick's collarbone.

Zing.

Nick's nipples are suddenly very much joining the party.

Nick groans and drops his head back. It hits the wall, and he doesn't care. He presses a hand against the back of Jai's head and shoves him into position. Jai makes a low, satisfied sound. His tongue laves Nick's left nipple.

Nick stares at the washing machine on the other side of the room, and at the container of laundry detergent sitting on top that promises the whitest of whites. Holy shit. Jai is licking his nipple because Nick pushed his head there. And—oh my God—now he's sucking it. If Nick weren't about to come in his pants, he'd probably be panicking a little about the weirdness of this. As it is, he shivers and holds Jai's head closer and tries not to think about Renaissance paintings of the Virgin Mary nursing Baby Jesus.

Fuck his brain, seriously. Why would it even go there?

And then Jai bites, actually *bites*, and Nick's brain shorts out due to sensory overload.

"Oh my fucking God!"

His mouth still works though. It's never needed his brain to function. Ask anyone.

Jai's fingers make quick work of Nick's fly, and then his jeans and underwear are being tugged down to his knees, and speaking of knees, Jai is suddenly dropping to his. There's a wet-sounding *pop* as Jai disengages from Nick's nipple, and he shudders as the air turns Jai's spit cold. But he's only got a fraction of a second to process that before Jai's lapping at the head of his dick.

Bye-bye again, brain.

Nick squeezes his eyes shut, breath hitching, fingers scrabbling for purchase in Jai's too-short hair. He's definitely not going to last. Definitely not. But then, who cares? It's not a fucking competition.

The sound of the basement door hitting the wall is as sharp and shocking as a gunshot.

"Jai? Have you seen— Holy *shit*. My bad!"

So.

So Nick's leaning up against a wall with his jeans and underwear around his ankles, and his wet dick flapping in the breeze. This is very probably exactly as mortified as Jai felt when the foreman wrenched the porta-potty door open.

Except the guy standing on the steps is not the foreman from Mr. Grover's site.

Oh sweet, squishy mother of Cthulhu.

The guy standing on the basement steps is Mr. Green, Nick's former history teacher.

"Jesus Christ, Ronny!" Jai exclaims.

Mr. Green's eyes are as wide and disbelieving as that time Nick told him the answers on his history test couldn't actually be wrong because there were an infinite number of timelines in the multiverse. It had been worth a shot, right?

Nick scrabbles to hitch his jeans and underwear up.

Well, this is awkward, Nick wants to say. Instead he just gapes at Mr. Green and wonders who's next. His childhood dentist? The woman who babysat him when he was six? His mom? Seriously, who?

"Nick," Mr. Green says.

"H-hey, Mr. Green."

Jai's head snaps back around, and he stares up at Nick. "Oh Jesus. Really?"

Nick can't answer him. He's thinking about more important things, like does this basement have another exit? Or a self-destruct button? Either would be sweet.

"Sorry," Mr. Green says, holding his palms up. "Sorry, guys."

He retreats up the steps, still staring, like a guy unwilling to turn his back on a wild animal.

The door snicks shut.

Jai climbs to his feet. "Nick, fuck, I'm sorry about that."

"No, it's okay." Nick's tongue feels weird and heavy in his mouth, and his skull feels like it's been stuffed with cotton. "Just . . . weird? Yeah. Weird."

Jai puts a hand on his shoulder.

"I think I want to go home now, Jai," Nick says. "Like maybe pick this up some time when my balls can actually crawl out of my body again?"

Jai's expression softens. "Yeah. Yeah, no problem."

Nick shuffles over to pick up the motorbike helmet.

His second ride of the night isn't as fun at all.

Nick: *Has anyone ever sucked ur nipples?*
Devon: *???*
Nick: *Is it weird?*
Devon: *I don't think so. Nobody's ever done it to me, but sometimes I pinch them when I'm jerking off, so?*
Nick: *Are we both weird?*
Devon: *Probably. Sounds like u had a fun night?*
Nick: *It was pretty ok. Also, so Mr. Green, our history teacher?*
Devon: *Yeah?*
Nick: *He saw my dick.*
Devon: *Wow. What? Wow.*
Nick: *IKR?*

CHAPTER TWELVE

"Nick Stahlnecker," Ronny says over breakfast the next morning. "Holy shit."

"Wait, who?" Kat asks, sliding into her chair and stealing a piece of toast from Ronny's plate.

"Jai is dating one of my ex-students," Ronny tells her. "He only graduated last month."

"He's eighteen," Jai mutters. "And we're not dating."

"Oh, you really should go with dating," Ronny tells him. "It sounds slightly less creepy than the alternative."

"Come on," Jai says. "He's your ex-student, not mine. He's legally an adult."

"Nick is one of your students?" Janice asks, appearing in the doorway. Her dressing gown is flapping open, revealing her slip, and her wet hair is drying in weird ways. "Ha! That's hilarious! You're dating one of Ronny's kids!"

"He's an *ex*-student, and he's eighteen!" Jai shoots back. "And we're not dating! And, Jesus Christ, Ronny, can you learn to fucking *knock*?"

He's still pissed. Not because he really blames Ronny, but because he texted Nick last night and still hasn't heard back. Maybe Nick's embarrassed. Embarrassment doesn't seem to quite suit the guy who offered to blow him in a porta-potty, but it doesn't have to be logical. Ronny was his teacher. It's probably right up there with a parent walking in.

"What happened?" Kat asks eagerly.

"Fuck you guys," Jai grumbles into his coffee, while Ronny mimes frantically at Kat, fist up to his mouth, tongue pushing his cheek out.

"So who was giving it?" Kat asks.

"*I* was," Jai snaps. "Okay? I was!"

Janice stands behind him and massages his shoulders. "Oh, honey." Her sympathetic tone would be a lot more believable if she weren't so obviously trying not to laugh.

"Aw, that's nice," Kat says. "You guys can totally bond over how it feels being busted with a dick in your mouth."

Ronny grins. "Actually—"

Kat elbows him. "One time, Ronny, that was *one* time! Shut up!"

"Oh, do tell," Janice says, and Jai wonders what it would be like to be part of a normal, sexually repressed family.

He stands, disentangling himself from Janice, and crosses the kitchen to put his coffee mug in the sink. "Yeah, I'm glad you all think it's so hilarious. Too bad Nick's not answering my texts, or I'd invite him over to join the laugh-fest."

The smile drops right off Kat's face. "Jai, I'm sorry!"

"Yeah, man," Ronny adds. "We didn't know it was serious."

"It's not," Jai says, leaning back against the sink. He shakes his head. "It's really not."

He's probably just going to keep repeating that until he believes it.

Jai: *Sorry about last night. Are you ok?*
Nick: *Yeah.*
Jai: *Do you want to meet up after my shift tonight?*
Nick: *It's Sunday though?*
Jai: *Do you have plans?*
Nick: *No, it's cool. Pizza Perfecto?*
Jai: *See you there.*
Nick: *:)*

Jai's old Timberlands did not come back from Vietnam in the healthiest condition. It's no surprise, really. He got three years of almost constant wear out of them. They're not the cheapest brand of boots out there, but they're the best he's found so far for backpacking. He heads to Walmart before his shift at Pizza Perfecto, to find a replacement pair and grab some new socks while he's at it. Now that he's working again, Argentina is back in reach.

Jai's halfway to the shoe department when he spots Nick.

He's standing in front of a display of storage boxes, looking half-asleep and fairly despondent, while beside him a woman loads up a cart. The woman has to be Nick's mom. She's a little shorter than he is, and has the same dark eyes and expressive mouth. Her hair is a shade or two lighter than Nick's. She wears it pulled back in a messy ponytail.

Jai thinks about slinking past, but it's already too late. Nick looks up and sees him: cue a shy, rueful smile and a blush that makes him look instantly sunburned.

"Now, we'll need at least three," the woman says. "This one has a broken lid. Help me get the— Nick, are you even listening to me?"

Nick starts.

The woman turns around and sees Jai. She smiles politely.

"Um," Nick says, scratching his head. "Mom, this is my friend Jai. Jai, this is my mom."

"Marnie," his mom says, eyes widening slightly. "It's nice to meet you, Jai."

"Nice to meet you too." Jai shakes her hand and wonders how much she knows. Has Nick even mentioned him at home? As either the not-a-boyfriend or the guy he blew on a construction site? Neither of those is much of a recommendation for parents, he supposes. He glances at Nick, hoping to take a hint from him. He should have known better.

Nick looks like a deer in headlights.

"Buying boxes?" Jai asks, and immediately hates himself. But at least he's contributing more than Nick.

"For college," Marnie says. "I keep telling Nick he'll need more than he thinks, but he just doesn't listen. You need storage boxes, Nick. You have more stuff than you know."

Nick mumbles something that sounds like "ant backpack."

Marnie ignores him. "Are you in college, Jai?"

"I never went," Jai says, and catches the way she looks at his Pizza Perfecto shirt.

So does Nick.

Jai knows he doesn't owe Marnie, or anyone, an explanation, but he can't pretend it doesn't rankle either.

"Actually, Jai *travels*," Nick says. "He's been to over forty countries."

"Oh," Marnie says, her expression shuttering. "How nice."

Nick huffs, jams his hands in his pockets, and chews his lip.

"It was nice to meet you," Jai says, and retreats.

Jesus.

Why does he get the impression that this isn't the first trip Nick and his mom have made for storage boxes? Maybe if they keep looking, Marnie will find exactly the right one to stick Nick in.

Okay, so maybe that's not fair. But Jai hardly knows Nick at all, and even he can tell the kid's freaking about his future, and picking out storage boxes isn't exactly helping him.

Jai's checking out the various boots when Nick finds him.

"Sorry about my mom," he mutters. "It's just she's really going to town on all this college stuff, and I don't even know if that's what I want, you know?"

Jai picks up a pair and checks the soles. Not great. "Have you told her that?"

Nick screws up his face. "It's not like I *don't* want to go. Jesus, I don't know. But it's just . . . What if this is all there is, you know?" He gestures.

"What, Walmart?" Jai asks with a slight smile.

"*Yes*, Walmart," Nick hisses. "Walmart, and boxes, and lists, and getting a job, and being a grown-up, and having a student debt and maybe not *even* a job, and then it's like you're locked in and maybe you never even figured out what you wanted to do in the first place!" He stops to draw a breath, and looks a little surprised at his own outburst. "I've maybe been reading *Catcher in the Rye* way too much lately."

"I can tell," Jai says. "When it comes to the soul-crushing meaninglessness of life, though, I much prefer Vonnegut's *Slaughterhouse-Five*."

"Isn't that about aliens and a teapot?"

"Only superficially."

"Oh." Nick reaches out and strokes the toe of a hiking boot. He sighs. "It's not like I can tell them though, is it? It's like I'm kicking against the cage, except there *is* no cage. And even if there was a cage, I'd be one of those animals that's too scared to leave it anyhow, because if I don't go to college, what else is there?"

"There's a whole world."

Nick snorts like he said something funny. "Yeah, no. That's not really my jam."

"There must be somewhere you want to go."

Nick twists his mouth. "Middle Earth?"

Jai laughs.

"Anyway," Nick says. "Sorry about before, and yeah, that's my mom. She's totally figured out we're fooling around, by the way, in case you didn't pick up on the disapproving mom-glare. Also, if it comes up, I might have told her you were twenty. You can totally pull that off, actually. She also wants me to invite you to dinner, because I haven't figured out how to work the whole 'fuck buddy' thing into conversation, so."

"So you're inviting me to dinner?" Jai asks, stomach clenching.

"Oh, God no! Not that— Well, you know." Nick stares at the floor for a moment before looking up again. "Wow. Who'd have thought anything could be more awkward than last night, right?"

"Right," Jai agrees.

"If you were my boyfriend, I would totally invite you to dinner," Nick says, "because you're hot like the sun. But that's not what we're doing here."

"Right," Jai says again.

"Right," Nick echoes, relief flooding his features. "Okay, so I'll see you later tonight, okay?"

"Okay."

"Okay, cool." Nick shoots him a grin and scurries away.

Jai loses sight of him somewhere in men's clothing.

At work, Devon is on cloud nine.

"Got the shovel talk," he says proudly when Jai asks. "From Ebony's dad. He sat me down and reminded me that he's a cop and knows where to hide a body. It was so cool!"

Nick's friend is as odd as Nick.

"No, see, because he knows I'm serious now!" Devon exclaims. "That's how it works. I promise to be respectful and not a dick, and he promises to kill me if I fuck it up."

Behind him, Ebony rolls her eyes. "It's bullshit!"

"It's tradition!" Devon exclaims.

"A bullshit patriarchal tradition where I get treated like a piece of property instead of a woman capable of making her own decisions," Ebony says.

Devon beams at her.

"Do you think he gave my brother's girlfriend the shovel talk?" Ebony asks. "No, of course not. Because people still think that a woman's sexuality is something to be controlled by men, and that if women have sex, we somehow lose value."

"That is fucked up," Devon agrees, his brow furrowing slightly even though his smile loses none of its brilliance. "But, like, for a man of your dad's generation, isn't it also a way of him expressing how much he cares for you?"

"My dad was born in 1972," Ebony tells him. "My grandmother burned her bra. He should know better."

"It was still kind of cool," Devon says, and Ebony snorts. "Anyway, I know that if I'm ever dumb enough to screw up with you, it's not your dad I have to be scared of."

"Damn straight." Ebony grins and moves past them with a tray of drinks.

Devon exhales slowly. "Wow. I am learning so much about male privilege lately. It's more complicated than I thought at first. Dude, do you even know how good we've got it?" He shakes his head slowly. "So, anyway, last night when I was getting the shovel talk, I figured that someone should probably give you one."

Jai raises his eyebrows. He leans back on the counter and folds his arms over his chest. "Okay. Let's hear it."

Devon nods sharply. "Okay. Well, Nick is my best friend in the whole world, and I know you're not like serious or anything, but he did cry in *The Force Awakens*, so." He shudders. "Okay, so did I, but that's not the point. The point is that Nick's a great guy, and he has feelings about stuff, and if you do anything to hurt him, I'll..."

Jai waits.

"Well, I really didn't think this through. I'm not a cop, and I don't know how to get rid of a body, and you could totally take me in a fight. Okay, so if you hurt Nick, I'll tell everyone on Twitter and Facebook *and* Tumblr what an asshole you are." He tries for a scowl. "And Instagram."

"Oh no," Jai deadpans. "Not Instagram too!"

"Dude," Devon says beseechingly.

"Fine. Consider me intimidated."

"Cool." Devon enters a phone order on the register. "Just . . . yeah, he's my friend."

Jai nods. "I get it, Devon. Really."

Devon looks relieved.

Jai heads to the kitchen to see what the delay is on table four's order. When he gets back again, Nick is at the front counter, eating a breadstick.

Jai nods to the back booth, and Nick heads on through.

It's surprising how quickly Jai has started to feel comfortable here, with Devon and Ebony and the others. And with Nick. He's as much a fixture of the place as the red-and-white checkered tablecloths and the raffia bread baskets.

"Staff special?" Jai asks him when he's finished with table four.

"What is it tonight?"

"Meatlovers with anchovies and pineapple."

"Eugh. Whose bright idea was that?"

"I'm blaming Tyler."

"There is actually no such thing as bad pizza," Nick says. "That's a scientific fact."

"Well, this one will test your precious science. I had one bite during my break, then went to Subway."

"I like a challenge," Nick declares. "Bring it!"

Subway is still open when Jai finishes his shift. He and Nick head over there, and Nick orders a meatball sub with as many extras as will fit.

"Dude, Tyler is a *dick*," Nick says, devouring his sub in the parking lot.

"Believe me, everyone has told him that tonight."

"Damn it!" A meatball lands with a *splat* on the cracked asphalt. "I doubt even the raccoons will eat that pizza."

Jai laughs.

"So," Nick says around a mouthful of sub, "I was thinking tonight we could, like, have sex?"

"Is that what you want?" Jai asks, heartbeat quickening.

Nick nods and swallows. "Yeah. And I thought maybe you could top me?"

Shit. The image sends a jolt of heat right through Jai. It settles in his balls. "Okay."

"Because I thought the first time it would be easier if, like, you could do it to me, and then I'd maybe know what I was doing if, um, if you still want me to do it to you later."

Jai is sure that if it weren't dark out here, he'd be able to see Nick was bright red. He can't wait to see the flush extending all the way down his body. "Yeah."

"Cool." Nick wraps his unfinished sub up and clutches it tightly. "So, this time we'll lock the door, right?"

Jai laughs. "Hell yes!"

"Awesome." Nick's voice wavers but he grins. "Let's do this thing!"

They head for Jai's bike.

CHAPTER ⬤ THIRTEEN

The couch is folded out into a bed.

Nick lies on it, naked, feeling both braver and more terrified than he ever has in his life. His meatball sub sits heavily in his belly, and he's worried he's going to throw it up. He's also worried he's too scrawny, his feet are too hairy, his balls are, and should he have shaved or waxed or something? None of the twinks in porn have much body hair. Is he an otter instead? That's a thing, right? Otters. Except now he's thinking about actual otters. Actual otters are adorable.

Then Jai is lowering himself onto the bed beside him, and Nick can't think about anything at all. The springs squeak a little, and the thin mattress dips, and suddenly they're making out, which is just the same as they've done a few times, except there is much more nakedness involved.

Nick tries to lose himself in the heat of Jai's touches. Tries to open himself to the kiss, but it feels so laden, and his anxiety is still clinging to him, edges sharp. He's also really fucking hard, and it's a small miracle he doesn't come the second Jai's thigh brushes against his dick.

He wants to say something maybe, to break the tension, to try to laugh off how obvious it is that he's so fucking nervous, but there aren't any words he can even imagine that can do that trick. And Nick has never been short on words in his life. It's more than nervousness. It may even be actual fear. Not just because this may hurt—how can it not, right?—even though Nick trusts not everyone in porn is faking how good it gets, but he's also scared he'll be bad at this, so it'll be awkward afterward, and he won't be able to look Jai in the eye ever again, and it will ruin everything between them. Not that . . . not that there's anything between them. Right?

Oh, fuck his brain, seriously.

Nick angles his face for a heady kiss, eager to distract himself from his own thoughts and lose himself in sensation. Jai hasn't shaved today, and the prickle of stubble around his lips feels rough and exciting. He's kissing a man. Not just a boy, although of course boys are awesome, but a *man*, with all the scratchy body hair and developed muscles to prove it.

The springs squeak again as Jai shifts and reaches over Nick. When he leans back again, he's holding *stuff*. A condom and a bottle of lube. The *snap* of the lid is as loud as a gunshot as Jai thumbs it open.

Nick has played with lube a bit. He ordered a dildo online once, and knew better than to put it anywhere near his ass without slicking it up first. But maybe he used too much, because he couldn't get a good grip on it, and when he tried to slide it inside him, it shot out the other end of his fist instead and hit the collectible Aragorn figure on the bottom of his bookshelf. The next time he tried, with less lube, he could only get it part way in, and then worried for ages that there was something wrong with him. Maybe he's too small there or something. Maybe one day a proctologist will discover that his ass is some sort of medical anomaly and nothing longer than an inch can fit up there. His ass will be famous in medical circles.

Except . . .

Nick shudders as a lube-slick finger rubs over his taint and presses against his hole.

Except Jai's finger slips right in.

Holy. Mother. Of. God.

It doesn't feel good, exactly, but it doesn't feel exactly bad either. It feels *weird*. It also feels a little like he needs to shit. Which, gross. But it's okay. As long as he doesn't shit and Jai doesn't end up with a handful of it, it's going to be fine, right?

"Okay?" Jai asks in a low voice.

Nick squirms a little, and could this be more awkward? Bad enough Jai has a finger up his ass, but now he wants to initiate a conversation as well? "Uh-huh."

"Tell me if you want to stop," Jai says, and kisses him.

Nick closes his eyes. He tilts his hips up and opens his legs a little wider. Says with his scrawny, hairy, inadequate body what he can't with his words: *Yes. Keep going. Do it.*

Which is not clear and explicit consent, probably, but this isn't an after-school special. Nick isn't always so great at talking about his feelings, unless it's with Devon. And this is even worse, because it's like feelings, but wrapped up in sexual things, like *needs*, which makes it a million times more potentially humiliating. Because how is he supposed to know what to ask for, or what to refuse, when he doesn't know exactly what's going on? Okay, he's seen porn, a lot of porn, and he knows what Jai's doing, but just because he can feel the stretch and the strange ache as Jai gets a second finger inside him doesn't mean that in any reality in any universe he would ever be comfortable with saying the words "finger" and "my ass" in the same sentence, whether it's to ask for more, or to ask Jai to stop.

Nick feels a sudden flash of fear at that realization. Is Nick really the sort of person who'd let someone go as far as he wanted because Nick was too embarrassed to tell him to stop? God. Maybe he is.

He opens his eyes again.

Jai's gaze is steady on Nick's as he slowly stretches him, and Nick forces himself to relax. Okay, Nick may be the type of guy who'd rather get pressured into full-on sex than have to awkwardly tell someone to stop in the middle of things, but Jai is obviously not the kind of guy who's going to push him.

It's okay. It's fine.

"Nick?"

"Yeah," Nick says, a little breathless with fear, but also with relief that Jai asked. "I'm okay. Keep going."

Wow. Good. So he doesn't need to actually say, *Please keep your fingers in my ass*, in order to give consent. That's incredibly reassuring to discover.

Jai kisses him again, then shifts back slightly. The muscles in his arm cord as he turns his hand, changes the angle of his fingers, and—

Zing!

A wild burst of pleasure shoots through Nick like lightning.

Hello, prostate. Nice to finally meet you.

Wow. That's just . . . wow. All the things are happening right now. Nick's not exactly sure he can even differentiate between all the battling sensations coursing through him, and it seems easier to just go with them, wherever the hell they're taking him. He's here for the experience, but he never expected the experience to feel quite this . . . weirdly hypnotic? Jai is totally putting him into some kind of freaky trance with his magic fingers. It feels really, really good, and it's making him kind of dozy. But also, more please?

He thinks he mumbles something like that when Jai helps turn him over onto his belly.

Foreplay is supposed to be a good thing. Except right now Nick feels like it's dragged on for hours and he is more than ready for the main event. The sheet underneath him is already soaked in sweat, and Jai's still just fingering him. And he needs to stop that, immediately.

Nick squirms.

His legs are spread wide, his aching dick absolutely leaking into the sheets, and probably the mattress, and he's totally wrecked even though he hasn't even come yet. And if Jai wants him to have enough energy left to actually participate in the main event and not just lie there like a dead fish, then Jai needs to get his fingers out of Nick's ass right now and put his dick in there.

He mumbles something like that into Jai's pillow and grinds his dick against Jai's mattress.

"What?" Jai stills the fingers inside Nick's ass. His other hand, splayed over Nick's damp lower back, keeps making small, comforting circles.

Nick lifts his head. "I said I'm not a finger puppet, Jai! Just put your dick in me already!"

Jai laughs. "Okay. Get your knees under you, yeah?"

Nick struggles to get his heavy, clumsy limbs to obey. It should be humiliating, waiting with his ass in the air—and totally on display—for Jai to fuck him. Except Nick is way past humiliation. He just really, really wants to come. Like every other time he's wanted to come in his life has nothing on this moment. Because Jai has teased him for what seems like forever, and Nick is eighteen, okay? He can rub one out in the shower in under thirty seconds if he has to. Instant gratification is kind of his specialty. But *this*? This is all new to him, and it's like torture and should totally be illegal.

He twists his neck as he hears the crinkle of foil, and watches wide-eyed, jaw hanging, as Jai rolls the condom over his very erect, very angry-looking dick. Nick's mouth waters like he's Pavlov's dirtiest dog. And then Jai is up on his knees behind Nick, his hands on Nick's hips, drawing him closer. Nick feels heat first, as their bodies almost touch. A wall of warm air that compresses as Jai closes the distance between them, and their damp, sweaty bodies finally meet.

He shivers.

Jai takes a hand off his left hip, and Nick's extensive study of porn tells him that this is it. That Jai is getting into position, getting his dick at the right angle. This is the moment Nick's been waiting for. It's *terrifying*.

Nick exhales shakily as the hot, blunt head of Jai's dick rubs against his slick, aching hole. And then it's pressing inside him.

Sweet Baby Zeus. Jai is *inside* him, and, okay, foreplay is apparently not overrated at all, because this doesn't hurt—it aches as Jai's dick stretches him, but it doesn't hurt—and the roadblock Nick hit that time with the dildo? Jai's incredible dick pushes straight past it.

Nick's breath shudders out of him, and he whimpers.

"Okay?" Jai asks, his voice hardly more than a groan.

"Y-yeah." Nick gets his elbows under him properly and arches back, and, oh wow, that's a lot of dick inside him. He has the sudden urge to press a hand on his stomach and see if he can feel it about to burst out of him. Like in *Alien*, but also kind of hot. "Are you all the way in?"

"Almost."

There's a part of Nick that worries he isn't ready for this. There's another part of him that knows he'll never get someone as ridiculously gorgeous as Jai Hazenbrook again. Both of those parts could use some work on their self-esteem, probably. But this is what Nick came here for, right? This is what hooking up with Jai is all about: losing his virginity so he knows what to do once he gets to college and maybe even starts dating someone.

Nick sucks in a breath. "Keep going."

His head is swimming, and it's almost like he can't get enough oxygen. He's aware of intense pressure, and shifts his body to try to ease it, but there's actually no escaping it because there's *a dick inside his body*. All Nick can do is bear down—thanks, internet!—and wait for his body to get used to it. Of course it totally helps when Jai hits his prostate again.

Nick groans as pleasure sparks through him. His erection, which had flagged a little when Jai pushed inside him, is suddenly back again and paying a lot of attention to the proceedings. Nick still feels more pressure than pleasure, but his dick is an optimist. It's pretty sure there's a happy ending on the cards.

It's good, okay? Also weird and new and a bit strange, but it definitely tips toward the "Praise Jeebus!" end of the scale. A part of Nick wants to lose himself completely in this, while the other part of him—the part that his mom took to get tested for ADHD that one time, because he had the attention span of a goldfish and six million different tabs open in his brain—is busy cataloging in detail each tiny sensation so he can dissect every moment again later in his head. And also wondering how soon he can text Devon and let him know he finally got a dick in him. Because Nick's been waiting a long time for this. Devon was sixteen when he first got laid, a year and a half ago. A whole year and half while Nick stewed jealously in his virgin juices. Which, ew, gross.

Jai drags his hand down Nick's spine, and Nick arches into it like a sweaty cat. Then Jai slides his hand underneath Nick and grabs his dick, and *bam*, Nick's brain is right back here on the page, and will never, ever be distracted again, no sir.

"How's that feel?" Jai asks, his voice straining, and Nick almost laughs, because how does it *feel*? The hottest guy in the world is fucking him and jerking him off at the same time. It feels like goddamn Christmas!

"Good," he groans out instead, rocking back into Jai's thrusts. "Fuck. 'S good."

Jai hits his prostate and squeezes his dick at the same time, and should Nick be thinking about presidents or state capitals or baseball statistics right now, or does he not care if he blows in under three point five seconds?

The second one.

Fuck.

The second one.

He comes, in a crazy explosion of bodily fluids, muffled obscenities, and the sort of jerking spasms that wouldn't look out of place on the dog when she's dreaming of chasing squirrels. He whines like the dog as well, because Jai isn't finished yet and everything feels weird and oversensitive, and Nick is suddenly too wrung out to actually contribute, thanks very much.

Then Jai is gripping his hips tightly and sort of shuddering into him, and yay, he's coming too.

Nick sags onto the mattress and resolves to start doing ab crunches and stuff from now on. Because stamina is a thing he could use, apparently. Jai still has enough energy to climb off the squeaky mattress and pad away. Nick actually kind of wants to watch him and get an eyeful of that naked ass, but moving seems like too much trouble right now.

He hears the blast of water in the laundry tub, and a few seconds later Jai is back with a damp washcloth, and he's wiping Nick's ass.

Nick squirms and snorts, and can't decide if that's really sweet or really weird. He's eighteen. That's plenty old to take care of his own ass maintenance, right?

"You okay?" Jai asks, leaning down to press a kiss to the back of his shoulder.

The small touch makes Nick flood with warmth. He lifts his head and turns it to gaze at Jai. "I think you broke me. In a totally good way."

Jai smiles. "You wanna watch a movie?"

Nick rolls over at last, flushing. "Okay."

He wonders if he should get dressed to watch the movie, but Jai doesn't make a move for his clothes so Nick doesn't either. Jai just tugs the sheet up so that he's not resting the laptop on his exposed dick, and Nick leans close and repays him for the life-changing sex by introducing him to the brilliance that is *Attack on Titan*.

It may just be the greatest night of Nick's life.

Nick: *Anus is an ugly word, right?*
Devon: *Um . . . Do I need to ask why you're thinking about aniseed?*
Devon: **anuses. Fucking autocorrect.*
Nick: *Jai fucked me tonight. It was so good!*
Devon: *Way to go, bro!*

Nick: *Like at first I was worried it would be bad and awkward and I would just let him finish so at least one of us could have a good time, but then it turned out great.*

Devon: *Wait, what? You would just let him finish?*

Nick: *Yeah, but it turns out I'm ok at asking for what I want, so it wasn't even like an issue.*

Devon: *That's good, I guess.*

Nick: *IT WAS AWESOME!*

Devon: *I'm trying to be supportive but please don't tell me all the details.*

Nick: *What? You'd never let a girl do butt stuff to u?*

Devon: *Maybe?*

Nick: *U totally should. Ur prostate is ur best friend, Dev.*

Devon: *But I already have an annoying little best friend.*

Nick: *I will fight u, bro.*

Devon: *:D*

CHAPTER  FOURTEEN

J ai texts Nick the next day to see how he's doing, and gets back an emoji of an eggplant. It's followed up by a thumbs-up, so Jai decides it's basically positive. He spends the morning clearing weeds from the overgrown back garden, then works the slow Monday evening shift at Pizza Perfecto. Devon's not working, and Nick doesn't show up. Jai's not too worried, since Nick texts him at least every hour with some random joke, cat meme, or *Attack on Titan* trivia. It's past midnight when he closes up and heads home. He sleeps like the dead.

On Tuesday morning he stays in bed until he hears his mom leave the house, and then gets up to go scrounge up some breakfast. He makes it to the kitchen just as Ronny is leaving.

"Got an interview?" Jai asks him.

"Got a *job*," Ronny says with a wide grin. The tight lines in the corners of his eyes that Jai is accustomed to seeing have eased this morning. "I've got a new assignment over in Springboro because one of their summer regulars broke a leg. Which sucks for her, but thank God, you know?"

"Good for you," Jai says.

"Thanks!" Ronny pecks Kat on the cheek and kisses Noah on the top of the head before he heads for the door. "Bye, Caden!"

"Bye, Daddy!" Caden yells back from upstairs.

The front door slams shut.

Jai sits at the table.

Kat slides a mug of coffee across the small kitchen table to Jai, and fixes him with a speculative stare. It reminds him of when she was eleven and had just discovered their mom's dog-eared collection of Trixie Belden books and decided that she too could solve mysteries. "So Nick stayed pretty late the other night."

Jai shrugs.

"You like this boy," she says at last, gaze sharpening.

Jai sips his coffee. "Of course I like him."

He's not in the habit of sleeping with people he doesn't like. Who would do that?

"No, you like him, like him," Kat presses.

He huffs out a breath, quirks his mouth into something caught between a grin and a grimace, and shrugs again. "I don't like him, like him. I just like him. It's a casual thing. He's fun to hang with. We're friends."

"Uh-huh. Sure, little brother." Her voice might be deadpan, but her eyebrows clearly don't believe him. She sets a plate of toast on the table in front of him.

Jai has never been more grateful for the distraction of two sticky little hands on his knees. He reaches down for Noah and hauls him onto his lap. Noah burbles happily to himself and smacks his hands on the table, sending cutlery clattering.

Jai tears a crust off his toast and gives it to Noah to gum on, and Kat gets Noah's oatmeal ready.

Crusts and crumbs and smears of butter and jelly on the kitchen table. Coffee and juice and spills and splashes. Jai kind of likes the domesticity of it all. Of course it helps that he can always hand Noah straight back to Kat if he wants a break.

Which is what he does the moment Noah gets his oatmeal and decides to start painting the table with it.

Kat sits down and takes Noah onto her lap, and Jai slides the oatmeal over to her to deal with instead.

"You like this boy," she says again, smirking.

Jai chews on a piece of toast. "Remember when we were teenagers and you were so good at ignoring me that half your friends didn't believe you had a brother? Good times."

"Sure," she says, holding a spoonful of oatmeal up for Noah. "Remember that time you carved my initials into Dad's new garden bench so I'd get in trouble?"

"Remember that time you smashed a mirror over my head?" Jai teases.

Kat rolls her eyes. "You were such a little baby about that!"

He laughs. "Hey, you were the one who burst into tears because you thought you'd get seven years of bad luck! I only cried because I had glass in my scalp."

"Oh, please," she says. "All the girls and boys like a rakish scar! You should totally thank me."

He rubs his head almost unconsciously. With his hair buzzed short, the narrow, jagged scar on his crown is visible. It's never bothered him, although he remembers his mom fretting about it when it happened, since he'd had a huge bald patch shaved into his head for the stitches. His dad had just shrugged and called him "Friar Tuck" for a few weeks.

He smiles at the memory.

"I'll bet Nick likes your scar." She waggles her eyebrows.

Jai snorts. He doubts Nick's even noticed it. Nick seems to have a lot of difficulty raising his gaze much higher than Jai's abs, to be honest.

"He's a cutie," she says. "I approve."

"Okay, I'm pretty sure I don't need your approval," he says. "And how would you know he's cute?"

"I heard you leaving to take him home on Sunday night." Kat bounces Noah on her knee as he begins to grizzle. "I might have peeked out the window."

Jai thinks of the way Nick sits behind him on the bike now. He's a little more relaxed than he was that first time. He likes to link his fingers together around Jai's abdomen and lean against his back. It feels good. "Yeah, he's cute."

"And you like him," she says, jabbing Noah's spoon in his direction. "Like him, like him."

"Really, we're back to that?"

"We never left it, Jai," Kat says with a grin.

Jai rides his bike out of town, feeling the drag of the wind as the buildings and houses slip away. About thirty miles out, there's a spot his dad used to take him to. It's just a curve of the river, with nothing special about it except that it holds the memory of so many long afternoons sitting with his dad, just talking.

They called it fishing, but half the time they left the rods in the truck.

Jai parks his bike off the road.

When he was a kid, there was no path here for cyclists and walkers. Now it's another place among millions where the smooth concrete means it's impossible to leave footprints. It's still nice though. Birds dive for insects skittering across the surface of the river. The wind encourages the trees to dip their branches toward the water. The day is a little hazy and warm.

Jai crosses the bike path and walks down the slope of the riverbank. He sits in the dry grass and watches the water.

He imagines his dad sitting beside him, and imagines the things he might tell him.

It's been years, but it's not the sort of pain that vanishes. The sharper edges of it have softened over time, and it's become a dull ache. It's not a raw wound anymore, but it will always be scar tissue.

He thinks back to Kat's teasing at breakfast, and wonders what his dad would have made of this thing with Nick. His dad was always the quiet one of the family. Jai takes after him in that respect, he supposes. Maybe his mom is right and he's an introvert too. He's never thought of himself like that before, but he does like to take time for himself, to sit and think.

It's weird, then, that he likes Nick.

Nick is everything Jai is not. Nick is loud. Nick has no discernable filter. He's smart, but he's also scatterbrained. He has energy levels that can only be attributed to a diet full of caffeine and sugar. By rights, Jai should find him exasperating. Instead, he finds him oddly charming.

Jai smiles and toys with a strand of grass.

He's fun.

Nick is *fun*.

And Kat is right.

Jai *likes* him, likes him.

"Jai!" Devon exclaims when Jai walks into work that afternoon. "Pool party, my place, Saturday night. You're off, so are you coming?"

Jai hesitates for a moment.

"Nick's coming!" Devon says with his easy smile. "Well, I haven't asked him yet, but he'll totally be coming. It's like the last party I'll get to throw before college. Everyone's going to be there."

"Okay," Jai says, figuring he can always sneak out again if he hates it.

"Great!" Devon slaps him on the back. "My mom and stepdad will be away, and since the last thing Lewis used the pool for was so his pastor could come over and, like, adult baptize people, I'm counting on you and Nick to get in the water and really gay it up."

"Gay it up?"

"Yeah." Devon's smile widens. "I need you guys to use your rainbow mojo to neutralize all the fundie that got put in the water when the pastor blessed it."

"You and Nick are as crazy as each other," Jai tells him with a shake of his head, even while a grin tugs at the corners of his mouth.

"We really are." Devon beams. "Hey!" he yells into the kitchen. "Where's the extra mozzarella sticks for table five?"

Jai heads to the back to shove his helmet in his locker.

Devon is ridiculous. Rainbow mojo? It's no surprise at all that he's Nick's best friend. They are obviously twins who were separated at birth.

Jai is waiting tables tonight, and hoping he'll see Nick at some point. Why wouldn't he? Nick's attached to Devon at the hip, and since Devon's working, Nick is sure to show up. Jai is a few hours into his shift when the bells on the door jangle and Nick steps inside. He heads over to the counter to fist-bump Devon, then turns his gaze on the restaurant area.

His face lights up when he sees Jai, and Jai smiles in return.

He thought it might be awkward—well, more awkward than Nick usually is—but Nick just slides into an empty booth and grins when Jai approaches him.

"Did you know there's a Pizza Hut in Japan run entirely by cats?"

Jai considers that for a moment. "That can't be true."

"It's called Pizza Cat," Nick tells him. "You can look it up."

"I'm probably not going to do that."

"You have no soul." Nick sets his phone on the table. "What's the staff special tonight?"

"Meatlovers with a burned crust and cheese that was one day past its expiration date."

"Sounds great!"

It really doesn't, but who is Jai to judge?

It's quiet enough that Jai's able to grab a few minutes and slide into the booth across from Nick after he fetches his pizza from the kitchen. Nick grins and flushes when Jai taps a foot against his. His smile eases some of the tension Jai didn't even know he was carrying. Last night was Nick's first time, and an emoji of an eggplant wasn't exactly explanatory.

"How are you doing today?" he asks.

"Good," Nick says through a mouthful of pizza, then narrows his eyes suspiciously. "Wait, do you mean like emotionally, or like how is my ass doing?"

Jai snorts. "Um, either, I guess."

"We are both good," Nick says. "My ass and me. I mean, there was a minute when I was looking at my bike seat wondering if I really wanted to come here tonight, but . . ." He shrugs. "Free pizza."

"Right," Jai says, feeling like Nick has dodged the second part of the question entirely. "Free pizza."

Nick's flush deepens, and he ducks his head briefly.

"Are you going to be hanging around until I finish?" Jai asks.

Nick wrinkles his nose. "Ugh. My mom wants me home by nine. We have 'college stuff' to do." Air quotes. "She wants me and my dad to write a weekly budget and lock in which meal plan I'm going to get."

Nick is wearing that same haunted, hunted look he gets whenever he talks about college, and Jai feels a stab of sympathy. He remembers that sensation of being trapped, but never by his mom. She knew he was desperate to get out of town. She worried about all the trouble he could get into while traveling, but she never tried to stop him. Probably because she knew it wouldn't have made a difference.

When Jai was Nick's age, he had already left Franklin behind. He'd already been halfway around the world, surrounded by people whose language he couldn't understand. He'd thrown himself into the strangeness of being on the outside, being the other. He'd relished it. At eighteen, Jai would have turned his lip up at the thought of staying in Franklin to work at a pizza place, or even going away to college. A small town full of small minds, or years in the drone factory of further education. He felt nothing but contempt for both options, and for anyone who didn't see it the way he did.

He was an asshole at eighteen.

Travel broadened his mind in unexpected ways. He knows he was a dick. He knows that just because other people don't enrich their lives the exact way he does, doesn't mean their lives are shallow and pointless. He learned not to judge, not even the people who look like him and speak with a Midwestern twang. That was the hardest thing.

He grew up.

Nick, picking the burned crust off his pizza, still has a lot of growing up to do.

Jai wonders what Nick will be like when he's done and, for the first time, feels a little sorry that he'll probably never know.

"Rain check, I guess," Jai says, standing up to get back to work.

"Yes, rain check!" Nick agrees, and then frowns. "That's a dumb expression. What does it even mean? How can I speak Elvish and not know English?"

"How can you speak *Elvish*?" Jai asks.

"Um, nerd alert, hello." Nick gestures to his Planet Express T-shirt.

Jai leaves him, laughing, and grabs a couple of menus for the family who has just walked in.

When Jai gets a chance to look at Nick again, he's engrossed with his phone.

Jai: *Pizza Cat was a viral marketing campaign for Pizza Hut.*
Nick: *What? Why r u trying to crush all my dreams? Also, u totally looked it up!*
Jai: *Because I needed to make sure I'm not living in a crazy world where cats make pizza.*
Nick: *Scared they'll put u out of a job?*
Jai: *Don't be ridiculous. Everyone knows that's what robots are for.*
Nick: *Lol! Good night.*
Jai: *Good night.*

CHAPTER FIFTEEN

On an otherwise innocuous Wednesday morning, Chris Stahlnecker announces his plans to ruin Nick's summer.

"Nick," he says, frowning at him over his breakfast. "Go and get dressed. You're coming to work with me."

"What?" Nick gapes. He shouldn't even be out of bed yet. He was up until three in the morning on Tumblr. "Seriously?"

"You have twenty minutes to get ready," Chris says.

Wow. Okay. Working with his dad. It's a fantasy Nick grew out of when he was about four, actually. It's been at least that long since he used to wave at his dad from the driveway every morning and complain to his mom that he wanted to go to the office and play with Daddy all day. "Playing with daddy" definitely has some weirder porn-related connotations these days. Which was skeevy at first, but luckily Nick developed some hard-core denial to combat his cognitive dissonance, which made it possible to get off on daddy porn without thinking of his biological father. It's been smooth, sticky sailing since then.

"Nick," his dad sighs. "Twenty minutes."

"Right!" Nick hurries upstairs to leap into the shower.

It's closer to twenty-five minutes before he's stumbling downstairs again, hair wet, button-up shirt sticking to his back a little. His dad doesn't comment on his tardiness though. He only opens the door and ushers Nick toward his car.

Nick settles into the passenger seat, hauling his phone out to text Devon about this latest disturbing development in his life. This feels a little like an ambush, which is fine, except does his dad think that Nick needed to be ambushed? Like if he'd spoken to him beforehand that Nick would have made up some excuse to get out of it? He probably would have, he guesses. Maybe? He doesn't really know.

"Jesus," Chris mutters as he backs the car out into the street, "it's like you're surgically attached to that thing."

Nick glances from his phone's screen to his dad. "Um, I was just telling Devon that we couldn't hang later today."

His dad grunts.

Nick watches their neighbors' yards slide past the window. "So, is this like a whole summer thing?"

His dad's hands tighten on the steering wheel for a moment. "That's the plan."

"Okay." Nick's stomach sinks. "Um, what will I be doing, exactly?"

"You can answer phones with Charlene, and do some filing. Then we'll see."

"Oh, so the same stuff I did at Mr. Grover's," Nick says, and his dad winces a little. Nick thinks of the porta-potty incident and winces as well. "Well, not *everything* I did there, just, um, office-related stuff?"

He's kind of looking forward to getting another stapler, to be honest. Staplers are fun.

"Just office-related stuff," Chris repeats, the corners of his mouth turning down.

Nick stares fixedly at the screen of his phone again.

There is probably never a time when his parents are going to find the blowjob thing funny. Which is a shame, because Nick feels it has the potential to be comedy gold. A real ice-breaker at parties. He bites his lower lip to hide a grin as he imagines someone seeing him and Jai together—this is for comedic purposes only, okay? It's not like it's going to happen or anything, or that Nick *wants* it to happen— and saying, *So, how did you two meet?*

It's funny, right?

Nick wonders if his dad would crack a smile about it if it was someone else's kid instead of his own.

The drive downtown seems interminable. His dad isn't even listening to the radio.

"Mom tells me she met your boyfriend," Chris says when they stop for a red light.

"Oh, yeah." Nick feels a stab of guilt, and he's not sure if it's because he told his parents he had a boyfriend when he doesn't, or if it's because maybe a tiny, secret part of him sort of wishes that . . . No, he's cool. He's being grown-up, right? No strings and all that. Except the other night with Jai was so great that Nick can't help imagining what it would be like to be Jai's boyfriend. Maybe it wouldn't be that different from what they're doing now, or maybe they'd actually spend the night together, and cuddle and stuff.

And then he feels guilty for even thinking about cheating on his cuddle-bro Devon.

"Jai, was it?"

"Yeah." It's like this red light is never going to change.

"What does he do?"

"He works at Pizza Perfecto," Nick says, and his dad gets that same dubious look his mom did in Walmart. It rankles. "Actually, he *travels*. For like nine months of the year, and then he comes back here in the summer and works. He's been to a bunch of places. It's pretty cool."

Chris raises his eyebrows a fraction and taps his fingers on the steering wheel. "And what are his plans for the future?"

"He's going to Argentina."

"I meant, what does he want for a career?"

Nick shrugs. "Hashtag YOLO?"

Chris looks at him with a frown.

Nick sighs. "I don't know, Dad. Why am I getting the third degree? We're messing around, okay? We're not getting *married*."

"So it's not serious?"

"No, it's not serious," Nick mutters. "I'm going to college soon, remember?"

"Of course," his dad says, and something like relief crosses his face. Then the light turns green and they head downtown.

Nick: *I have a job?*
Jai: *Congratulations?*
Nick: *It's with my dad. Hella awkward.*
Jai: *What does your dad do?*
Nick: *He's an accountant.*
Jai: *And you love math so much.*
Nick: *Ugh. Kill me now. Please.*

Charlene isn't as much fun to work with as Patricia was, Scrabble obsession and weird tea fetish aside. The problem, Nick decides, is that Charlene has known Nick since he was a baby. He suspects she even babysat him a few times. Of course she treats him like a sweet little apple-cheeked kid. She changed his diaper more than once. She's nice, but she's not as surprisingly filthy as Patricia often was.

But Nick does get a key to the office supplies closet, so this job definitely has an upside. He not only gets his own brand-new stapler, he also starts a collection of different-colored Post-it notes in the top drawer of his desk. By lunchtime he's used them to make an *Attack on Titan* flipbook, and storyboarded the next episode of his web comic.

Accountancy is exactly as exciting as construction was, and Nick doesn't even have Jai Hazenbrook's perfect ass to look forward to.

Except, like, he totally does.

Okay, so it's not like Jai is going to brighten his day by walking into the office and giving Nick something to ogle, but, on the plus side, Nick is now actually allowed to touch his ass. And also his abs. And also to kiss him and blow him, and do all the things. *All* of them. And the reality completely eclipses the fantasy in every way.

Nick chews on the end of his new pen—he has twelve—and daydreams about everything he's going to do with Jai at Devon's pool party on Saturday night. Disturbingly, most of his fantasies seem to involve the people he went to high school with mistaking Jai for his actual boyfriend. *Oh yes, look what the short kid dragged in, fuckers.*

This is already the best summer ever, and it's only going to get better.

Because—Nick squirms in his chair—because Jai said that Nick can top him, and that is kind of awesome and incredible, right? And if it feels even half as good as bottoming, then Nick is going to love it.

He writes himself a list.

1. *Research topping.*
2. *Buy lube like a grown-up. Lots of lube.*
3. *Research prep!!!!*
4. *Attempt to last longer than 30 seconds when you put your dick in the hottest guy in the universe.*

Look at him, prioritizing like an adult. His dad would be so proud.

But, also, probably he wouldn't be, so Nick waits until his half-chub subsides, and takes his list to the shredder and disposes of it carefully. Then he sits at his desk again and stares at the motivational poster of a raindrop on the opposite wall and worries that maybe he lied to Jai the other night at Pizza Perfecto. Not about his ass. His ass is fine. But about his emotions?

Nick has emotions, and he's not entirely sure what to do about them.

The raindrop poster doesn't offer any clues.

Neither does the scuffed carpet that Nick turns his attention to next.

He fiddles with his phone for a while, curling the springy cord around his finger and then pulling it straight and then letting it go again so it grabs him like a little coiled tentacle. Then he glances over to where Charlene is pretending not to glare at him, and stops fucking around with the phone.

After lunch he steals another pen from the office supplies.

He calls it Gloria, and decides that it's his favorite.

"This is nice," Marnie says, her smile a little too bright. "Eating dinner together, like a family."

Nick drags his fork through his mashed potatoes and hopes the sound he makes is an agreeable hum.

"How was work, boys?" she says, and Nick silently prays she's not being cute. He and his dad going to work together? That's not cute. It's awkward and horrible, and the more time they spend together, the less they have to say to one another.

It's his dad's turn to hum.

"Good," Nick lies, because his mom deserves at least the semblance of a conversation, right? She's trying so hard, he almost feels embarrassed for her.

Her smile ratchets up a few more uneasy degrees. "Oh, that's *great*! What did you learn today?"

Um . . . that he'd rather slit his own wrists than become an accountant?

"Like phone stuff?" Nick says hesitantly. "And Charlene showed me how to schedule appointments and stuff."

None of it was exactly rocket science, but Nick still screwed most of it up at least once. He's sure Charlene is dreading tomorrow just as much as he is. There is nothing spiritually redeeming in office work. Even the free office supplies can't make up for the soul-crushing horror that is an office job. Except what else is there? Nick is allergic to the sun and the outdoors, and despite his crazier fantasies of completing his criminology degree and getting a job in law enforcement, what are the chances he'd *not* accidentally shoot himself with his own firearm? Nick knows his limits. He's just not so sure of his strengths.

"That sounds good, honey," Marnie says, and pushes the dish of beans toward him.

Nick can take a hint. He scoops some onto his plate.

"Um, so can I get my car back now?" he asks. "Devon's having a pool party on Saturday, and it would be cool if he didn't have to swing by and pick me up first."

His dad glances at him. "We'll see."

Which is probably as good an answer as he's going to get.

Nick nods and eats his beans.

And then fucks everything up after dinner.

Everything.

He's on Skype with Devon, and he thinks his parents are downstairs watching TV. And he forgot to close his door.

"It was horrible, Dev! I thought I was going to die of boredom! Seriously, twenty years from now, if I'm as boring as my dad, you have to promise to kill me quick and put me out of my misery, okay?"

"Nick—"

"I'm not even kidding!"

"Nick!" Devon looks horrified.

"What?" Which is right when Nick's attention is caught by movement in his own little Skype screen. He spins around on his chair just in time to see his dad stepping back from the doorway, his expression tight. "Oh fuck. Oh fuck fuck *fuck*."

"Bro," Devon says, and then sighs. "Fuck, *bro*."

Fuck indeed.

Nick: *My dad hates me.*

Devon: *Did u talk to him?*

Nick: *No! ARE YOU CRAZY?*

Devon: *Ignoring it won't make it go away, Nick.*

Nick: *I literally asked you to kill me if I turned out like him. There is no good way to spin that.*

Devon: *Don't spin it then. Just say sorry.*

Nick: *I don't think that's going to cut it.*

Devon: *Dude, u can't just ignore it.*

Nick: *Can I come and stay with u?*

Devon: *. . .*

Nick: *He HATES me and I'm a horrible person.*

Devon: *You're not a horrible person.*

Devon: *Mostly.*

Devon: *Sometimes.*

Devon: *ILY.*

Nick: *Also, Mom said I don't need to go to work with him tomorrow, so I think I won?*

Devon: *That's not winning, bro.*

Nick: *Just. I don't know when it got so bad with us?*

Devon: *Ur dad isn't as bad as you think. I will swap u for Lewis.*

Nick: *Lewis isn't as bad as YOU think.*

Devon: *I will swap u for my real dad.*

Nick: *No thank you.*

Devon: *See? Ur dad isn't so bad. So man up and apologize before he grounds u for the weekend and u don't get to rub yourself all over Jai in my pool.*

Nick: *Good point. ILY too, Dev.*

CHAPTER  SIXTEEN

Devon lives east of the river, a few streets away from Franklin High School, on Clearbrook Drive. It's the sort of uniform suburban neighborhood that Jai kicked back against so hard when he was growing up, and he still feels a prickling sense of something like claustrophobia when he turns onto the street. He wonders if it's the proximity to the high school—a place he's avoided successfully since graduating—that brings those old feelings up again. Or the fact that he's going to a party for teenagers.

Yeah. Probably the second one.

The party is in full swing by the time Jai arrives. The house is packed with kids holding red Solo cups. The pool is even more packed. There's music thumping from the stereo, and it's kind of chaotic. Jai finds Nick hanging by the snacks. He straightens up when Jai approaches him, eyes already a little glazed.

"Hey, Jai! You made it. That's awesome!"

Jai doesn't drink that much—he prefers to get stoned when the opportunity arises—but he takes the cup of beer that Nick offers him, and reflects for a moment on his life choices. Even when he was a teenager, he didn't party like this, so what the hell is he doing here now?

Is it possible he's a twenty-five-year-old curmudgeon?

Then Nick grins at him, and something inside him eases a little.

Jai knows a few of the guests from working at Pizza Perfecto with Devon and Ebony, but most of the crowd seem to be from Devon and Nick's graduating class. Listening to them, Jai gets the impression that Nick wasn't exactly popular in school. Everyone loves Devon and seems to sort of tolerate Nick.

"Who is *that* guy?" one kid asks when Jai's not quite out of hearing range. "No fucking way is Stahlnecker banging someone like that!"

Jai doesn't think Nick heard, but he puts an arm around him just in case, because fuck that kid.

Nick grins up at him, nose wrinkling. "Hey."

"Hey again."

Nick snort-giggles. It's ridiculously cute.

The heart of the party seems to be the pool, but there's a secondary group in the large living room. The walls are papered in something hideously floral, and a velvet painting of the Last Supper takes up most of the wall above the TV. Someone has taped a pair of black-rimmed glasses to Jesus's face.

"It's bullshit!" Ebony exclaims as they approach the group.

"What's going on?" Nick asks.

Ebony rolls her eyes. "These guys want to play Seven Minutes in Heaven." She rounds on the group. "We're supposed to be adults, not high school freshmen!"

One of the other girls grimaces. "It's just a bit of fun, Ebony!"

"Fine." Ebony picks up the two mixing bowls full of scraps of paper. She tips the contents of one bowl into the other, and mixes them around. "Who wants to play now?"

"I'm still game," the girl says, hands on her hips.

The first two names drawn are Stephanie and Anna. The girls in question look at one another, shrug, and head for the closet. Ebony sets the timer. A few of the kids chatter excitedly, but Jai figures there's nothing happening behind the closet door apart from two straight girls counting down the clock.

Hipster Jesus doesn't look impressed.

Nick takes him by the hand and leads him toward the kitchen. "Did you ever play Seven Minutes in Heaven?"

"No." Games like that are one of the big reasons Jai avoided high school parties. Forced interaction with another person with the added bonus of potential humiliation? Not something Jai sought out. "I never went to many parties."

"Really?" Nick screws his face up. "But you're *hot*!"

"And curmudgeony," Jai tells him.

Nick grins and bumps his shoulder against Jai's. "No way, dude. You're all Zen, and you, like, exist on a different plane from the rest of us. We're all these soulless robot consumers, and you're sitting somewhere contemplating the sunset and the meaning of the universe. Or the meaninglessness. Jury's still out on that one."

He's an idiot. Jai kisses him for it.

"Nick!" someone yells as they enter the kitchen. It's Devon. He's drunk too, or well on his way there. "Nicky!"

They hug like it's been years since they saw one another, instead of, most likely, minutes.

"Hey, Jai," Devon says with a brilliant smile. "It's cool you made it, man! I was worried Nick would be a total wallflower, and I don't know if you've noticed the decor, but the last thing this house needs is more fucking wallflowers."

Jai snorts at that. "Yeah, I noticed."

"Ugh. My mom's taste is terrible." Devon grins again. "Have you guys seen Ebony?"

"She's in the living room, hating on Seven Minutes of Heaven for being heteronormative, I think," Nick says. "She mixed all the boys' names and girls' names together."

Devon's smile softens into something sickeningly smitten. "She's so incredible." Then his smile vanishes and he grips Nick by the neck of his T-shirt. "Am I a fuckboy?"

"What?" Nick slurps at his beer.

"You know. A fuckboy." Devon chews his bottom lip for a moment. "A *bro*."

"You're *my* bro," Nick says staunchly.

They fist-bump, and then Devon looks accusingly at his hand. "But seriously, like, am I a fuckboy? Like look at me. I'm white, I'm middle-class, and I'm from Ohio. I could not be more of an entitled douche, right? I reek of privilege, dude! I also say 'dude'!" His eyes grow wide.

Nick slings his arm around Devon's shoulders. "Devon, you are not a fuckboy. You're an overthinker. Fuckboys don't overthink anything. Fuckboys don't *think*."

"Are you sure?" Devon asks.

"Totally sure," Nick promises. "Also, maybe you should drink some water, okay?"

"Okay." Devon still looks a little anxious, but he pats Nick on the back. "Thanks, bro."

He heads off toward the living room.

"I should probably drink some water too," Nick says.

"Probably," Jai agrees mildly.

Nick stares into his cup for a moment. "After I finish this, I will."

Then he takes Jai by the hand and draws him upstairs.

"So, this is Devon's room," Nick announces, slapping his palm around on the wall near the doorframe until he finds the switch and the light flickers on.

"Are we supposed to be upstairs?"

"Please," Nick says, drawing Jai inside and shutting the door behind them. "I'm totally allowed in Devon's room whenever I want." He crosses to the dresser and hauls the bottom drawer open. He reaches over and pulls a T-shirt out, holding it up for Jai's inspection. "This is *mine*. I practically live here."

He bundles the shirt back into the drawer, closes it with his foot, and sets his cup of beer on the dresser. Then he reaches forward and tries to hook his fingers through Jai's belt loops. He misses, shrugs, and grabs Jai's hips instead, urging him over toward the bed.

Jai lets himself get pulled onto the bed, ending up lying on his side with his legs tangled in Nick's. He lifts a hand and places it on the side of Nick's face and kisses his beer-bitter lips. Nick sighs and his mouth falls open under the gentle pressure.

"I was totally going to ask if I could top you tonight," he whispers when Jai breaks the kiss. "Then I had some beer for, like, Dutch courage, and then some more, and now I'm so courageous I'm sort of seeing double, and I think if you had two asses I wouldn't know which one to aim for."

Jai laughs.

"I said that aloud, didn't I?"

"Yeah, you did."

"Whoops."

Jai kisses him again. "'S'okay. We've got plenty of time for you to top me when you're sober."

"We have like *weeks*," Nick says, eyes widening. "That's hardly any time at all. Then I'll be at college, and you'll be . . ." He wrinkles his nose. "Abyssinia?"

"Argentina."

"Close?" Nick hedges.

"Not even." Jai curls his hand over Nick's hip and rubs a circle with his thumb.

From downstairs and outside, the sound of the party is muted. The bass is a dull thumping heartbeat, and the shouting and laughter seems almost distant. It's quiet and peaceful in Devon's room, and Jai thinks he could probably fall asleep like this, with Nick curled against him. Then Nick is moving, a careless elbow hitting Jai in the chest. He's twisting off the bed like a cat mid-fall. A moment later he's back again, leaning against the headboard of Devon's bed with a laptop balanced on his stomach.

Jai sends him a questioning look and rests his head on Nick's shoulder.

Nick opens the laptop and enters the password.

"You know his password?"

"Please. We share the same brain."

"Huh." Jai watches the screen as the laptop boots up. "Who's using it at the moment?"

Nick laughs.

There's a folder on Devon's laptop labeled *NO, NICK, NO!*

"Straight porn," Nick says as the pointer hovers briefly over it. He selects the next folder instead: *MOVIES*. "Dev's got my back."

He clicks on a movie.

It's *The Fellowship of the Ring*. Jai has seen it before. It's okay. He'd never tell Nick that he's at best ambivalent about it, of course. That's sacrilege in Nick's world. And it's sort of fun to watch Nick watch the movie. Jai can see the tension ease in him the moment the Shire comes into view. He's rapt, his eyes wide. His mouth is hanging open a little, his bottom lip damp. Jai wants to lick it. He settles for shifting up and putting an arm around Nick instead, and letting Nick lean into him.

"I wish I lived in Middle Earth," Nick mumbles a while later as the hobbits set off on their quest. "I wish someone would come along to me and say, 'Nick, you need to do this thing. The fate of the world depends on it.' It would be good to have a purpose, you know? To be important."

Jai looks at him questioningly. "You think you're not important?"

Nick huffs. "I think I'm just the same as every other kid at this party. I think that when we're little, they tell us stories about being heroes and saving the universe, and then when we get older, they tell us to grow up and stop believing in dumb stories anymore."

"I don't think you're the same as every other kid here," Jai says quietly.

It's true. He flashes back to Kat— *"You* like *him, like him!"*—and ignores the burst of emotion in his chest that is half warm affection and half panic. Jai doesn't fall for people. He likes people, and he messes around with people, and he stays friends with people, but he doesn't fall for them. That's not in the plan at all.

"I don't know what I want to do," Nick says, his voice growing fierce for a moment. "I don't know what I want to *be*. I don't even know who I am right now, I guess, and everyone else seems to have it all figured out."

"I don't." Jai meets his worried gaze. "And I'm okay with that. Maybe one day I'll find some place I want to settle down, get a long-term job or whatever, but if I don't, so what? I like doing what I'm doing."

Nick sighs. "I feel like . . . I feel like I'm stuck in some weird feedback loop. Like here I am trying to rage against the machine or whatever, except there's nothing here to rage against. I get really angry and stuff, but I don't even know why. And I'm not *dumb*. I know that college is a good idea, but I just don't think I'm ready, and I don't want to go. And every time I imagine actually getting up the courage to tell my dad that, I either imagine him totally losing his shit or, best-case scenario, he says, 'Okay, Nick. If you don't want to go to college, what do you want to do?' And I don't have the answer to that!" The corners of his mouth turn down. "And what have I got to complain about, really? Nothing. I'm lucky, and I know that, but lucky isn't the same thing as happy, is it?"

"No," Jai agrees.

"So what do I do?" Nick asks, eyes wide and imploring. "What do I *do*, Jai?"

"I don't know." Jai shrugs, and they sit in silence for a while as the hobbits are pursued by the Nazgûl. "I really don't have my shit together any more than anyone else, you know? I'm not Zen, and the only reason I started traveling was because my dad died and I was pretty much a fuckup for my entire adolescence. You think you're kicking back against nothing? Jesus, you should have seen me. I thought that if I could get away from this town, it'd be a massive 'fuck you' to everyone from school, and that somehow I'd also figure stuff out."

"And you haven't?" Nick asks anxiously.

"Still working on it," Jai says. "But that's okay. I like traveling. It's the journey, right, not the destination?"

"You're totally Zen, actually."

"I don't think you know what that word means." Jai elbows him.

Nick smiles. "Probably not."

They lean against each other and watch the movie some more.

"Oh, this! This bit here!" Nick exclaims as the hobbits enter the tavern in Bree. "The first time I saw this, I was six, maybe? I totally fell in love with Strider."

Strider inhales on his pipe, illuminating the planes of his face.

Nick sighs, and the laptop on his stomach dips. "So hot."

Then, for some reason that can only be related to all the beer he's consumed, Nick starts to giggle uncontrollably.

Jai's not a fan of the movie, maybe, but Nick isn't wrong. He takes the laptop off Nick's wildly vibrating stomach and sets it on his own so they can keep watching.

Devon: *Dude!*
Devon: *DUUUUUUUDE!*
Devon: *Bro?*
Devon: *I saw yu go upstars with Jai!*
Devon: *You'd bettr not be gettng jizz in my bed.*
Devon: *I am srious!*

Devon: *Nickeeeeeeeeee!*
Devon: *I need my bed! Not doing it with Ebony in my parnts bed!*
Devon: *I hate you sooooo much rigt now.*
Devon: *Lube ad condoms in top drawer.*
Devon: *I still hate you thogh.*

CHAPTER ⬠ SEVENTEEN

Jai dozes off just as the Fellowship leaves Rivendell. Nick divides his attention between the laptop screen and Jai's profile at first, but then it's all about Jai's profile. He's so hot. And also smart. And also nice. Because he listened to all of Nick's earlier word vomit about quests and college and not knowing who he is, and not once did Nick get even a hint of "What the fuck is this kid *on?*" in his expression.

Nick is definitely getting too attached to Jai. On one hand that's incredible because, hello, Jai Hazenbrook isn't totally repulsed by him, and all the available evidence suggests that he'll even hang out with Nick when Nick isn't sucking his dick or stuff. On the other hand, it's going to make leaving a lot harder.

A lot.

Nick climbs off Devon's bed. He needs to pee. He drinks the rest of his warm beer first, and then heads for the bathroom. From downstairs he can hear the music thumping. The party sounds like it's still swinging. Maybe there are snacks left. Or beer. Nick probably doesn't need more beer. That's what his bleary-eyed reflection in the bathroom mirror tells him anyway, but what does that guy know? That guy's probably an idiot.

Nick washes his hands and heads downstairs, and somehow gets roped into the party again when Olivia, a girl he sat next to in the Model UN one of their teachers tried to set up—she was Sweden and he was Finland, and they did not do northern Europe proud—squeals and hugs him.

"Hey, Sweden!"

"*Hejsan*, Nick!"

Okay, so Olivia had maybe been a little more dedicated than Nick. Olivia wants to dance, so they head into the living room for a while. They dance, and Olivia tells him how she's going to college to be a pediatric surgeon, and Nick just gapes at that because who *are* these people who know what they want to do, and he is totally in awe of her, but were there classes or something on how to be a grown-up, and why was he not informed of them? It's very confusing.

The night wears on. They run into some other kids from the Model UN. Olivia ditches Nick to hook up with Australia. Nick drinks too much, but he's having fun. The whole party seems to be filled with this weird sort of desperate affection, because the clock is ticking down on their last summer together *ever*, and even if everybody wasn't always friends at school, or close at all, the looming loss feels momentous.

It's past midnight when Nick remembers Jai and heads upstairs again. He's had more beer. A lot more beer. He doesn't realize that anyone's followed him up the stairs until he's coming out of the bathroom again, and Logan is standing right there. Then Nick blinks, and Logan crowds him up against the wall, hands on his shoulders, holding him there. Nick's kind of wasted. He can't exactly focus his eyes right now. Or his brain.

Logan seems pretty sober. His mouth curls into a grin as he leans in close. "I hear that gay dudes give really great head, huh, Nicky?"

Nick scrunches his face. "What?"

He's aware that there's somebody else here now, and a square of light is cast on the wall of the corridor beside him. Devon's bedroom door is open.

Logan tightens his grip on Nick's shoulders. "You could totally help me out and suck my dick."

Nick's jaw drops. A spike of panic cuts through his gut, and this doesn't make any sense. Like none at all. Logan makes no sense.

"Okay." It's Jai. Jai is here. He steps toward them, looking all tall and strong and *pissed*, and pulls Nick away from Logan. "What the fuck is your problem?"

Logan shows Jai his palms, suddenly all innocent. "Just offering, dude. It's not like you guys are *together*, right? I mean, how could you be?"

That's when Nick becomes aware of a bunch of sniggering guys watching from the top of the stairs. His stomach sinks. He catches Jai's gaze, and he doesn't need to spell it out, does he? Great. Just how he wants to end the summer. With Jai witnessing this little display of homophobic bullying the guys have put together for old times' sake. Nick feels like he's a high school freshman all over again, and he's just been shoved into a row of lockers by some asshole in a letterman jacket. It's a total cliché, but so was most of high school, right?

Jai rolls his shoulders. He's at least half a head taller than Logan, and he's carrying a lot more muscle. "Actually, we are together, and if you ever touch my boyfriend again without his explicit consent, I'll punch you in the fucking face. Are we clear?"

Boyfriend! What! Nick's jaw drops.

"Dude," Logan says, reproachful, like Jai's taken this friendly joke completely the wrong way.

Jai leads Nick away, through the gaping spectators and down the stairs.

"Oh man," Nick says when Jai gets him outside. "What even just happened?"

Jai opens his mouth to answer, but Nick doesn't hear whatever he says because he's suddenly doubled over, vomiting beer on the lawn. A gaggle of bikini-clad girls squeals and runs away.

Jai rubs Nick's back and sighs. "Let's get you home, okay?"

"Okay," Nick says, breathless. "Oh no. Jai? I got sick all over my shoe."

Jai says he doesn't trust Nick to hold on, so he leaves his bike at Devon's house and they walk. Jai makes Nick drink from a bottle of water as they start off.

"Sorry," Nick mumbles about a hundred times before they've even cleared Devon's street. He has to stop again to vomit in the gutter. "Dude, I'm really sorry."

"You drank a lot tonight," Jai points out. "It happens."

"I shouldn't have pre-gamed it," Nick moans. "My dad is going to kill me. He already hates me, so." He gulps down some more water, and then his eyes widen. "I would never suck Logan's dick anyway! Not if he paid me! He's an asshole."

"That's the impression I got, yeah."

"His dick is probably tiny anyway."

"Miniscule," Jai agrees.

Nick snorts. Jai is awesome.

It takes about an hour to walk to Nick's house, mostly because they take it slow to give him at least half a chance to sober up.

"Have you ever done something really bad?" Nick asks, and then gets distracted by a letterbox in the shape of a barn. "Like, I don't mean killed a guy or anything, but just something that made you worry that maybe you weren't, like, a half-decent person at least some of the time?"

Jai is silent for a while. For a very long while.

"Holy shit," Nick whispers. "Please tell me you haven't killed a guy!"

"No, I was just trying to work through your words. I haven't ever killed a guy," Jai promises. He frowns. "What sort of bad thing are you talking about?"

Nick crunches the plastic water bottle. "My dad heard me telling Dev that I think he's boring."

"Boring?"

"It sounds dumb, I guess," Nick mutters. "But *boring*? I mean, it's like I can't even be bothered enough to hate him or something. He's just meh, blah, *boring*." The guilt churns in his stomach. Or maybe it's the beer. It's hard to tell at this point. "Devon says I should apologize, but Dad hasn't said anything, so maybe he didn't care?"

Nick can't look at Jai when he says that. He can't read Jai's silence, and isn't sure he wants to.

"Oh man," Nick says at last, squinting at a cat crossing a lawn. "Let's just keep walking, you know, and talk about other stuff, and you can forget I said anything about my home life and my shitty personality. Because, you know." He makes a face and shrugs.

"What do I know?" Jai asks. "Seriously."

Nick glances at him suspiciously. "Because you know that's not what this is about?"

Jai frowns. "What do you mean?"

"I mean we hook up," Nick reminds him. "You're not like my social worker."

"But we're friends, right?"

Nick squirms a little. "Um, yeah?"

"Then shut up and keep walking," Jai tells him with a smile.

"But you told Logan Littledick I was your boyfriend!" Nick exclaims, and claps a hand over his mouth. For a moment he thinks he's going to be sick again, but then the crisis seems to pass, and he removes his hand and sucks in a deep breath. "Or is that a thing I drunkenly imagined?"

"I told him that so he'd back off," Jai says. "And because he seemed to think we couldn't be dating."

"But we're not dating," Nick points out.

"No, but it's not like we *couldn't* be," Jai shoots back.

For a moment they both stand there in the dark stillness of the suburban street, staring at one another, and then a nearby dog goes ballistic and starts throwing itself against its fence. Jai reaches out and takes Nick by the hand, and they move on.

Nick isn't sure if he's in shock, or if he's too drunk to process anything much at all.

"You know what sucks most about tonight?" he asks when they finally stop in front of his house. "Apart from the vomiting."

"What?"

"It was a pool party, and we never even went for a swim." Nick blinks at Jai under the glow of the streetlight. "Jai! *I* have a pool! We should swim now!"

"I'm pretty sure you shouldn't swim when you're drunk."

"I think that's just after you've been eating," Nick counters. "And probably also just ocean swimming? Maybe lake swimming, if it's, like, a disgusting muddy lake. And anyway, you're still totally sober, so you won't let me drown, will you?"

"Nick..."

"Come on," Nick says. "I'm all sweaty and gross. A swim would be great."

It *is* a hot night, and Nick can see the exact moment when Jai folds. Nick grabs his hand and leads him triumphantly around the side of the house.

The side gate squeaks when Nick tries to open it silently, and he gets a fit of giggles. Everything is either tragic or hilarious tonight. Beer. Then Scooter appears out of nowhere, and snuffles happily against Nick's knees while he scruffs her.

"Hey, Scooter! I'm a scary burglar, and you caught me. Good girl! You are the best, yes you are!"

It's dark and quiet in the backyard, and the breeze is making tiny ripples lap against the edges of the pool. Nick ambles toward the water, pulling his shirt off as he moves. He hopes the silver moonlight works like a really kind Instagram filter and makes him look all flawless and ethereal. It probably doesn't, and even if it does, the effect is probably ruined when he almost trips over his jeans when he tries to tug them off without removing his shoes first.

He's a disaster, really. This cannot end well. That knowledge has never been enough to stop Nick from doing dumb things though.

Nick's wearing his trunks under his jeans. They're tight boyshorts, and he bought them specifically for Devon's party because Jai was going, and Devon promised they hugged his ass in a good way.

He steps into the pool and sits on the step for a moment before sliding all the way in.

"You coming in, Jai?"

"I didn't bring my trunks."

"Oh." Nick squirms a little bit, churning up the water as he peels his trunks off and tosses them. They land with a wet slap on the concrete beside Jai's feet. "Skinny-dipping time!"

Jai strips his clothes off and gets into the pool. Now *Jai* is ethereal and flawless. Totally.

It's dark and quiet and perfect. The stars are reflected in the rippling surface of the water, and Nick feels as though he's floating in the sky. And then Jai is close to him, breath warm, skin gleaming, and he pushes Nick gently against the side of the pool and kisses him. Nick hopes his mouth tastes like chlorine instead of vomit.

Nick moans and raises his hand to rub his palm against Jai's cheek. Water drips from his arm and into the pool again: a tiny, melodic cascade. Jai nips his bottom lip, and Nick huffs out a laugh and wraps both arms around the back of Jai's neck. He spreads his legs as Jai pushes into his space, and he hooks his ankles together behind Jai's thighs. Jai reaches down and lifts him, and their dicks brush together. The heat of their bodies and the cool of the water make Nick shiver.

"Oh my God," he whispers, tilting his head so that he can suck beads of water off Jai's neck. "We totally need to fuck in this pool."

Jai shakes his head ruefully. "I don't have a condom."

"Seriously?" He bites his lower lip.

"Yeah." Jai licks at the indentations Nick's teeth have left. "Sorry."

"You are the worst boyfriend ever," he says with a hesitant smile.

"I like it when you call me that." Jai kisses him again.

Nick cants his hips up, pushing their dicks together again. "Really?"

"Really." Jai gets a hand between them and wraps it around both their dicks. "You're cute and funny and ridiculous. And hot. So fucking hot."

"Oh, wow. I died of alcohol poisoning tonight, didn't I?" Nick asks, licking a stripe up Jai's cheek. "I'm lying dead in the hospital or something, because in no universe do I get to call someone as hot as you my boyfriend."

Jai ruts lazily against him. "Bullshit."

"It's like Frodo and Legolas getting together," Nick insists. "It just doesn't happen. Barely even in fan fiction. Hobbits stick with hobbits, just as nature and God intended!"

"Nick," Jai says.

Nick squints at him. "Jai?"

"Stop it." Jai leans forward and kisses him gently. "It was sort of flattering at first, but we know each other now. And if you just see me as some hot guy . . ."

"Oh jeez," Nick whispers. God. He's been such a dick to Jai. The last thing he ever wanted was to make him uncomfortable. And it's the last thing he ever expected as well, that Jai may be fragile in ways Nick can hardly even begin to understand. "I'm a horrible person, remember? I am shallow as fuck, but I promise I'm not objectifying you. Like I totally was in the beginning, because hello! And also you saw my poems. But I like you, I really do. You're like a good person and everything, and you're smart and you're kind, and I'm an asshole. Ask anyone."

"You're not an asshole." Jai rocks against him gently, and Nick gasps.

"I'm pretty sure I am." Nick groans and buries his face against Jai's throat. "Oh fuck. Please make me come."

"Um . . ."

"What?" Nick mumbles.

"Your dog is staring at me."

Nick twists around and flings a handful of water at the curious dog. "Scram, Scooter!"

Scooter pads closer to the pool and pants.

"Oh, that is so disturbing," Nick whispers. "Can we just ignore her?"

Scooter slumps down at the edge of the pool.

"We can just ignore her, right?" Nick closes his hand around Jai's and squeezes their dicks together.

"Yeah," Jai agrees, sounding a little breathless.

Which of course is right when the porch lights turn on, blinding them both.

Nick and Jai freeze.

"Nick?" the silhouette of a man asks. "Nick, is that you?"

Fuck.

It's his dad.

Devon: *Heyy bro! Did Jai get y home ok?*

Devon: *Bro?*

Devon: *Nick, I'm serius. Did yu get hme ok?*

Devon: *You wre pretty smashed, ad Ebny heard Logan was a dick to you. R you ok?*

Devon: **EBONY*

Devon: *OMG please don't be dead in a ditch.*

Devon: *Nick?*

Devon: *I'm caling yoou.*

CHAPTER  EIGHTEEN

"**D**ad, hey!" Nick exclaims.

If Jai could drown right now, that would be fantastic. Instead, he inches away from Nick and hopes to hell the water is dark enough to hide the fact they're both naked.

"Um . . . this is Jai? My boyfriend? Jai, this is my dad."

"Jesus Christ," Nick's father says when he gets close to the edge of the pool, and Jai realizes that no, the water is not dark enough at all. "Put some fucking clothes on!"

The man turns his back long enough for Jai and Nick to scramble out of the pool and back into their clothes. Jai is in hell, and all he can think of is how much Kat and his mom are going to die laughing when they find out. Because of course they'll find out. They always do.

Evil fucking witches, the pair of them.

Jai mans up when Nick's dad finally turns around again. Nick is struggling with the button on his jeans, and Jai resists the urge to help him. He's pretty sure putting his fingers that close to Nick's dick is not going to improve things right now.

"Mr. Stahlnecker," he says instead, and sticks his hand out. "Jai Hazenbrook."

"Chris," Nick's dad says, shaking his hand like he's half-afraid to touch it. Like he knows exactly where it's been tonight.

"Chris," Jai repeats. "I'm, ah, I'm sorry we had to meet like this."

Chris's face says he's more than sorry. It's the sort of expression that traumatized soldiers in war movies have. Or the sad dogs in ads against animal cruelty. It's hollow-eyed and blank, as though Chris Stahlnecker has seen things too terrible to relate.

Nick is still fumbling with his jeans. He's obviously drunk. Nowhere near as bad as he was at the party, but still a long way off relearning all his motor functions. He finally gets the button done up, and very slowly draws the zipper closed, one hand shoved down the waistband of his jeans to protect his naked junk.

Chris stares silently at the pair of them.

Jesus. Jai is twenty-five years old. He's had sex before. He's had good sex and bad sex, and funny sex and awkward sex, but he's never had sex that's been interrupted by his partner's father. Jai remembers the time he was crossing the border from Turkey into Greece, when the border guard hauled him away for questioning for something that, even now, Jai isn't sure about. He was twenty-one at the time, and all he could do was vividly replay scenes from *Midnight Express* in his head. He remembers getting robbed at knifepoint in Estonia. He remembers that train in India, and the way it screeched as it bounced right off the goddamn rails. Jai has been in a few situations where he's only had a split second to come to terms with his own mortality, to make his peace, to tell himself that whatever happens, it's *okay*. This is somehow worse than all of them.

"Dad—" Nick bites off whatever he's going to say, because at that second his phone starts blasting "The Imperial March." Nick looks surprised for a moment, then digs his phone out of his pocket and stares blearily at the screen before he taps it. "Dev, um, hey."

"Nick!" Chris glares at him. "Are you—"

"I'm gonna have to call you back." Nick ends the call and shoves his phone back in his pocket, and then meets Chris's gaze. "Devon was just making sure I got home okay."

He shuffles a little closer to Jai, and Jai straightens up.

He can't quite read the tension here. Nick's obviously seeking protection, but Jai doesn't know if that's because this is terrible and mortifying, or if it runs deeper than that. How did Nick describe his dad? Boring? That doesn't seem to fit with any ideas Jai is formulating that Chris Stahlnecker is a bully or abusive or a homophobe, but how can he be sure? Just because Nick is funny and ridiculous and outgoing doesn't mean it's not a mask.

It doesn't mean Chris Stahlnecker isn't beating the hell out of him behind closed doors.

How long was it before Kat told anyone about Caden's piece-of-shit dad?

"She's left him," his mom told him over the phone.

"She what?" He had to go outside to hear properly. The hostel was party central.

"Kat's left Gary." Something in Janice's voice sounded strangely fragile.

"Why?" Jai asked, already dreading the answer.

The guilt was something they both had to come to terms with afterward. Kat had never given any indication that anything was wrong, but still, shouldn't they have known? Shouldn't they have been able to tell?

Is Jai supposed to be able to tell now?

He puts an arm around Nick's shoulders, and meets Chris Stahlnecker's gaze. Not staring him down exactly, not challenging him, just . . . holding his ground?

Nick draws in a deep breath. "Dad, I'm eighteen, and Jai's my boyfriend. I'm really sorry you saw that, but I'm not sorry we did it."

Chris's expression shifts, and Jai relaxes. Okay, so he misread this. Chris is pissed still, but he's not violently angry. He looks almost vulnerable for a moment, like a man out of his depth, and then he nods sharply and turns away. He walks toward the back of the house without another word.

"Oh Jesus." Nick sags a little, his breath wheezing out of him. "Jai, you should probably go. I'll talk to you in the morning, okay?"

"Are you sure?" Jai asks him.

"Yeah." Nick steps away from him. He crouches down and picks up his wet trunks. He squeezes them out, and water splatters on the ground. "You've already rescued me once tonight. Any more and I'll start feeling like a Disney princess." His smile seems forced. "So, yeah, it's cool."

"Are you sure?" Jai asks him again.

"Um, yeah?" Nick looks puzzled for a second. His jaw drops. "Oh! No, I mean, he's pissed, but that's, like, the extent of it. My dad has never raised a hand to me, like, *ever*. I'm pretty sure that's where most people think he went wrong, actually."

Jai snorts and fights to keep his tone serious. "Okay, but if you need me, call me, okay?"

"Yes." Nick steps close to Jai again, and pushes himself up onto his toes to kiss him. When he steps back, his eyes are bright in the moonlight. Still largely unfocused, but bright. "Because you're my boyfriend, and you care about me."

"Yeah," Jai says, reaching down to twine his fingers through Nick's.

Nick smiles like everything is right in the universe. "Yeah," he echoes. "Good night, Jai."

"Good night." Jai squeezes Nick's hand quickly, and then heads down the side of the house. The squeaky gate clangs shut behind him.

It's almost three by the time Jai gets home. He has to backtrack to Devon's place to pick up his bike first, and he heads downtown to get takeout after that. It's late enough that he's surprised to see the light on in the living room once he makes it home.

"Hey," he says, leaning on the doorjamb with his helmet in one hand and his takeout bag in the other.

Kat blinks up at him from the couch. "Holy shit, please tell me you have fries in there."

Jai tosses her the bag, sets his helmet on the coffee table, and slumps onto the couch beside her. "What are you doing up at this hour?"

Kat digs through the bag. "Caden woke me up to tell me he couldn't sleep. Twenty minutes later he's snoring like a bear, and I'm the one with insomnia." She waves a hand at the television. "So I'm mainlining *Breaking Bad*, since I'm the only person in the universe who missed it the first time around."

"How is it?"

"It's okay." Kat shoves some fries in her mouth. "How was the party?"

"Fine. Nick got drunk, I took him home, and then his dad busted us naked in their pool."

Kat snorts so hard she sprays him in half-chewed fries.

"Gross!"

"Oh, Jai!" Kat starts laughing, and doesn't stop until she's gasping for breath. "What is it with you and Nick? It's an exhibitionist kink, right? Right?"

"It's really not, I promise." Jai pulls the cheeseburger out of the bag and unwraps the greasy paper. "I don't know what the hell it is though."

"How'd his dad take it?" Kat asks, wiping her eyes.

"About as well as anyone would, I guess." Jai opens his cheeseburger up so Kat can steal the pickles. "I mean, I'm pretty sure I'm not going to get an invitation to dinner anytime soon, but I don't think he's going to go ballistic on Nick or anything."

"You were worried about that?"

Jai shrugs. "Stuff like that happens."

"You bet your ass it does," Kat says wryly. She looks at him with her head tilted to the side when he struggles not to react. "You don't need to walk on eggshells around me, Jai. I can talk about abuse without breaking down in a hysterical mess, you know."

"Yeah, I know."

"Good." Kat eats another fry. "So. Nick. Where are you going with this?"

"Nowhere," Jai says around a mouthful of cheeseburger. He shrugs. "He's got college, and I've got Argentina. It was only ever a short-term thing. I mean, we'll stay in contact, I suppose. See where it goes if we're both back in town at the same time next summer. If he's still single and it's something he wants to do."

Kat raises her eyebrows.

"We haven't talked about it, okay? But I can't ask a college kid to be exclusive, can I?"

"I don't think I've ever heard you talk about being exclusive with anyone before."

"Yeah." Jai scrubs his knuckles over his scalp. "This is all uncharted territory. Tonight we decided we were boyfriends."

Kat's jaw drops. "Seriously?"

"It doesn't change anything."

"Sure." Kat punches him in the shoulder. "You keep telling yourself that, little brother."

Jai balls up the burger wrapper and throws it at her head. "Jesus, I'm tired. Enjoy your show."

"Leave the fries," she commands.

Jai flips her the bird, leaves the fries, and heads down to bed.

Jai's tired, but he can't sleep. He texts Nick to see if he's okay, even though he doesn't really expect an answer at this hour. He ends up reaching for his laptop and going online. He checks out the reviews for a few hostels in Buenos Aires, and then finds himself looking at pictures of Iguazú Falls. The falls look like one of those places too beautiful to actually exist, and he wonders if the reality will match his expectations. Often it doesn't, but that doesn't really matter. There's always something about a new place, even if it's just the fact Jai has never been there before, that is still magical.

He finds himself thinking of Nick again, and the look of wonder on his face when he was watching the opening scenes of *The Fellowship of the Ring*, as the camera panned over the Shire and the music swelled. Magic is however you find it, Jai supposes.

When he was a kid, Jai had a globe. It had been his grandpa's, he thinks. It was old enough that the USSR was still a thing. His mom had wanted to throw it out, but Jai had insisted on keeping it. A globe felt like something important. It was the sort of thing he'd seen in movies. Important people in important offices always seemed to have globes. Big, shiny globes set in dark wooden frames; nothing like the dusty, dented, plastic thing Jai had inherited. Still, he liked it. Nobody else he knew had a globe.

One night after his dad died, Jai found the globe at the back of his closet where he'd been looking for his weed. He took it up onto the roof—it was the only safe place to get high without his mom smelling the smoke—and spun it lazily around on its squeaky axis underneath the stars. He'd been itching to escape. Not to see the world, not at that time, but to put Franklin and his mom's tears and Kat's anger and this small, stale house that he sometimes imagined still carried the scent of his dad's aftershave behind him.

He spun the globe and jabbed his finger on it.

Portugal.

Okay. Well, at least he'd *heard* of Portugal.

A strange sort of excitement filled him in that moment. In the months since his dad's death, he'd been unanchored, restless, torn apart by grief, the remaining pieces not large enough to paper over the holes his dad's death had left in him. But now he had a purpose. Now he had *something*. He was getting the hell out of Franklin, and he was going to Portugal.

A decision made all those years ago shaped him, and is still shaping him. He isn't running anymore, isn't thinking about what lies behind him. He has his eyes fixed forward these days, open to the wonders of the world. Maybe he'll never settle anywhere—he feels restless just thinking about it—but that isn't important, because the world is an amazing place, and he needs to experience everything it has to offer.

He glances over to the corner of the basement. A smile tugs at the corners of his mouth when he sees his backpack and remembers Nick's astonishment at the size of it. He can only imagine the look of horror on Nick's face if he ever tells him about that time in Laos when he wore the same pair of pants for nine days straight.

Good times.

Jai stretches, yawns, and finds himself googling backpacks, even though he doesn't really need a new one. Shit, though, that one looks comfortable. And the detachable daypack has a fuck-load of extra pockets.

He may accidentally buy it.

Jai closes his laptop. When he's checking out backpacks like they're porn, it's way past the time to sleep.

He dozes off looking at his backpack in the corner.

It's also way past time to be sticking around Franklin.

Pauly: *Can you pick up an extra shift today? Devon called in sick.*
Jai: *Sure. What time?*
Pauly: *As soon as you can get here?*
Jai: *Ok. On my way.*
Pauly: *Thanks, dude! You're a lifesaver.*

Jai: *It's no problem.*
Pauly: *Goddamn unreliable teenagers.*

CHAPTER ✪ NINETEEN

The kitchen light is on when Nick gets inside the house. He takes a deep breath and walks toward it. His dad is filling a glass of water from the sink. He turns when he hears Nick.

"Jai," his dad says. "Harvey mentioned that name."

Whoops. Nick reflexively squeezes the sodden trunks he's still holding, and water drips onto his toes and the floor.

"Your boyfriend is the guy you got fired with."

Nick nods slowly.

"Jesus, Nick!" Chris upends his glass in the sink, then rakes a hand through his thinning hair. "You said you met someone at the pizza place. Why is everything with you a goddamn *lie*?"

"Because you don't want to hear the truth, Dad!" The words are out before Nick can stop them, and then they just keep coming. "Because you don't want to hear that I'm more of a fuckup than you know, and I do dumb things all the time, and I don't know how to grow up, and I don't want to go to college to get a degree that I'm going to mess up anyway, and end up with a job I hate!"

Chris flinches back. "You don't want to go to college?"

"No!" Nick flounders. "I don't know! I don't know anything, okay? I don't know *anything*!"

He's angry at his dad for making him say these things, but he's angrier at himself for feeling them. He *knows* he's a fuckup, but he's been trying so hard to pretend he's not, and of course he fucked that up too, because he's Nick Stahlnecker, and that's what he does. He fucks things up. It'll probably be on his headstone one day: *Nick Stahlnecker, fuckup*. He's like Holden Caulfield, but at least ten times more annoying. And also he doesn't have a cool hat. But other than that they could be twins. Whining little bitch twins.

God. He really should never have read that book.

He just . . . Nick just wanted to be special. He wanted to be Luke, with a destiny. He wanted to be Frodo, with a quest. He wanted to be an unlikely hero and do something that mattered, but there are no quests in the real world, where everything is much bigger and more tangled and complex than in the stories he loves. In the real world, small people don't get to be heroes, and Nick is the smallest person he knows.

"Nick," his dad says.

Nick waits for him to say something else, but apparently his dad's got nothing either.

"Sorry," he mutters. "I'm drunk and stupid. Sorry."

He turns and heads upstairs. A part of him imagines what it would feel like if his dad stepped forward and put a hand on his shoulder, maybe pulled him into a hug. And maybe Nick would say something like how he doesn't really think his dad is boring, just that what his dad does isn't for him, and maybe they'd actually talk stuff out, and things would be better.

But his dad doesn't reach out for him, so Nick guesses he'll never know.

He wipes the water off his face as he reaches his bedroom. If he's crying, he can't tell.

Nick: *My dad caught me and Jai naked in the pool.*
Devon: *DUDE!!!!!!*
Nick: *That's why I couldn't talk when u called.*
Devon: *He mad?*
Nick: *Not really. I don't think he cares enough to be mad.*
Devon: *He's probabbly still in shock tho?*
Nick: *Maybe. IDK.*
Devon: *R u ok?*
Nick: *Yeah. Going to bed now. Talk tomorrow?*
Devon: *For sure, bro. Call me.*

Nick falls asleep to *The Two Towers*. He doesn't even make it to the part where Aragorn and the others meet Éomer and the Rohirrim, which is legit his favorite scene in the whole movie. Beards. It's the beards. And all the manly posturing. And the leather pants. Really, it's a scene that works on every level. A fucking cinematic masterpiece.

He wakes up a little past dawn, hungover, feeling like every orc and cave troll from the Mines of Moria has taken a shit down his throat. He stumbles to the bathroom and is sick in the toilet. Then he crawls into the shower cubicle and sits under the hot spray until he feels like he's a tiny bit human again.

When he finally drags himself back to his bedroom, he finds a glass of water and a pack of Tylenol on his nightstand. He swallows two of the Tylenol and burrows under his comforter again. Sleep gradually softens the pounding in his skull.

It's morning proper by the time he resurfaces. The loudest birds in the world are shrieking in the tree outside his window, and the sun is unnecessarily bright. Nick hates everything, mostly himself. He thinks briefly about getting some breakfast, but his stomach warns him not to go there. Hell no. But more water would be good.

Nick slinks downstairs, only almost tripping down the stairs twice. He's going to count not breaking his neck as a win. He figures it's the best win he's going to get today, right? He tries to remember exactly what he yelled at his dad last night, and if it was as horrible as he suspects.

"What is even wrong with me?" he mutters to Scooter when she meets him at the bottom of the steps. She thumps her tail against the wall in answer. Scooter doesn't care if he's an idiot or an asshole. Dogs are the best.

Nick makes it halfway to the kitchen, and stops. He can hear the kettle burbling. The dull squeak of the fridge seal popping open and squeezing shut again. He can hear the low murmur of his parents' conversation. The sound of their voices makes Nick's churning stomach flip. Did he really *yell* at his dad?

It's not fair that's the flashback he keeps getting instead of the part where he was naked with Jai in the pool. If Nick could replay that in his sad, aching brain—cutting out the way it ended, of course— that would be just great.

He takes a deep breath and steps into the kitchen.

He regards his parents warily. "Hey."

It's weird. Nick thought he was used to the way his parents are disappointed in him. He thought it was nothing he couldn't handle. But this morning even his mom is looking at him like she isn't quite sure what she sees. Like somehow Nick is someone they don't know, as though just one more dumb decision—or the trifecta of his being drunk, naked, and humping a guy in the pool—is all it takes to push Nick from someone his parents don't really get and can't quite connect with, into someone who is a total stranger to them.

His sudden dizziness, Nick thinks, doesn't all come from his hangover.

"So, um," Nick says, glancing from his mom to his dad and back again. "I'm sorry about last night. It was hot and we were taking a swim and we got a little carried away. I'm sorry I was drinking, and I'm sorry I never told you that Jai was the guy from the site."

Mostly, Nick thinks, he's sorry that he has disappointed them. He hates how he's always saying sorry, then going and lying and getting busted all over again. It's such a stupid, obvious trap, but every time he turns around, he's still caught in it, and he knows he has nobody to blame except himself. Why is it so hard to tell the truth? It's just like whenever Nick tells himself that he's going to eat healthy and start doing crunches and get abs and stuff, but when he looks down again, he's somehow gotten his hand stuck in a bag of Cheetos. The truth shouldn't be so difficult. It shouldn't be so weak.

In stories, truth is always so *big*. It has the power to shatter the earth and reshape whole universes.

Harry Potter is a wizard.

Vader is Luke's father.

Neo is the one.

And what's Nick's truth? That he's scared of going to college.

Fucking pathetic. No way in hell does a truth like that deserve a close-up shot, an orchestral swell, and a tortured Mark Hamill screaming, "Noooooooo!" as he clutches at the stump of his wrist.

"'M sorry," he says again, his voice a dry croak.

His mom purses her lips. The skin at the corners of her eyes tightens up like the "before" picture for some sort of magic wrinkle cream.

His dad stirs creamer into his coffee and scrapes the spoon against the inside of the mug. He takes the spoon out and taps it three times against the rim, like the chimes of a tiny bell announcing the next round in the boxing ring. It's a fight that Nick is woefully underprepared for. The sort where he'll just sway, punch drunk, while his opponent gets in all the hits.

"How are you feeling?" Chris asks, which is not what Nick was expecting at all.

He shrugs, because he doesn't think his parents really want to hear about how much his self-inflicted hangover hurts. Like, he won't win any points by trying to milk it. Even if it is probably the worst hangover that anyone in the history of the world has ever suffered. Nick's pretty sure it is. Even thinking about blinking hurts.

His dad regards him briefly over the rim of his coffee mug before slurping some down and then setting the mug on the table again. "You should take some more Tylenol and get some more sleep."

No, this is definitely not what Nick is expecting. It throws his already struggling brain into confusion. He doesn't know what this is—if it's his dad making an overture, finally treating Nick like an adult who is allowed to make his own admittedly stupid decisions and suffer the consequences, or if his dad is setting him adrift somehow. Cutting his anchor rope and letting the ocean pull him away. Not coldly. Not cruelly. And isn't that what Nick wanted? Except maybe he's not ready to go yet. Maybe he's not ready to stop being a kid, even though it rankles every time his parents treat him like one.

"Yeah," he says and crosses to the fridge. He pulls out a bottle of water and turns it over in his clammy palms. "I'm really sorry," he says again, even though he's not sure what good it will do. He's not even sure what reaction he wants.

His dad's expression is as unreadable as before. "We'll talk about it later, Nick."

"Okay," Nick says. "Okay."

He retreats upstairs and back to bed.

Jai: *Everything ok?*
Nick: *I guess. I have the hangover from hell though.*
Jai: *I meant with your parents.*
Nick: *I know. Same answer.*
Jai: *Give me a call if you want to talk.*
Nick: *K. Will probably just sleep more though.*
Jai: *Ok.*

Nick sits on the end of his bed and stares at the neat stack of storage boxes in the corner of his room. He's supposed to be filling them soon and taking them to Ohio State, where there will be forms to fill out, and an assigned dorm room waiting for him, and timetables and classes and mundane things that for some reason he finds so fucking terrifying. He's going to be one of those kids who buckles under the pressure, he knows. Because that's what he does. This one time in junior year, he didn't prepare a talk he was supposed to give in English. So he skipped school that day. And then, because he knew he'd be in trouble for that, he skipped the next day as well, and the day after that. College is going to crush him. It'll be worse than all those times in high school, because this time Devon won't be there.

Nick's not stupid exactly. He's just . . . He's really bad at dealing with pressure. He's never told his parents that, because it's too late now and it will just sound like another excuse. He's never told them that sometimes he's not just dodging his responsibilities because he's lazy and forgetful. Sometimes he lies awake all night thinking about them, until they grow so large in his mind that he just . . . *can't.*

He's spent so much of his life pretending that he doesn't really care when he screws up that he's pretty sure at this point nobody will believe otherwise. Except Devon, probably. Devon knows Nick better than he knows himself. Devon absolutely knows that Nick isn't kidding when he posts the video of "Wind Beneath My Wings" to Facebook and tags him in it, even though they both play it like it's a joke.

No. No, Nick is absolutely not going to cope at college on his own.

He scrubs at his wet cheeks and tears his gaze away from the boxes. Stupid dumb boxes.

Stupid dumb Nick.

His mom comes up to check on him once, and he pretends to be working on his web comic. Instead he's just scouring the pad with his pencil, digging the point in so much that it leaves deep furrows in the paper.

"Nick?"

He stares at his pad. "Yeah?"

"Nick, if you didn't go to college . . ."

Her voice is more tentative than he's used to hearing, and he glances up before he can stop himself. She looks anxious, the lines across her forehead as stark as those he's leaving on the paper. She looks middle-aged. She is, of course, but this feels like the first time he's seeing it. When did those wrinkles appear in the corners of her eyes? When did that streak of gray in her hair show up? Why isn't she the woman he remembers from when he was a kid? They'd laughed a lot back then. He remembers she used to take him to the park, and hold him up so he could reach the monkey bars.

She purses her lips for a moment, and then her breath escapes her in a sigh. "If you didn't go to college, what would you do?"

That's the million-dollar question, isn't it? God knows he can't hold down a job.

"I don't know," he says, his voice catching. "I didn't know I was supposed to have it all figured out by now."

"Oh, Nick." She sits down beside him. "You don't have to have it all figured out."

Nick thinks of Olivia, future pediatric surgeon. He kind of hates her a bit, to be honest. All jealousy of course. Not because he wants to perform delicate surgery on even more delicate little human beings, but because Olivia's got a plan, and Nick could really use one of those.

"This isn't about your boyfriend, is it?" his mom asks quietly.

"What?" He snaps the point of his pencil in surprise.

"I mean, do you not want to go to college because he won't be there?" his mom asks. She's keeping her voice even, like this is dangerous territory and Nick is a wild animal she's managed to corner.

"Jai's got nothing to do with it," he says. "Honestly, Mom. This is how I've felt for a while now."

"You didn't say anything."

He shrugs. What was there to say?

His mom smiles brightly, but he can tell she's forcing it.

No, I will not let these clouds spoil my picnic. No, I will not admit the glass is half-empty. And no, my precious little angel is not skirting close to a complete mental breakdown when he thinks about the future.

"This is just nerves, Nick. Everyone feels like this, okay?"

"Okay," he echoes. Echoes are hollow, right? So are empty vessels.

Movement at the door snags his attention. His dad's gone the moment Nick catches sight of him, and Nick wonders how much he heard. Could have been worse. At least Nick didn't call him boring this time.

"Okay," his mom says, patting his shoulder. "Okay! I'll let you get back to your . . ."

They both look at his scoured sketch pad for a moment.

"To whatever you're doing here," his mom finishes.

Nick nods and picks up a fresh pencil. He drags the point across the page roughly, leaving a jagged scar behind.

CHAPTER  TWENTY

Jai doesn't see Nick again for a few days. They text, but it's a shallow form of communication, and Jai isn't sure how much he can trust Nick's assurances that he's doing okay, however many smiley face emojis he attaches to his messages. Jai is kept busy with work. Devon's not the only unreliable teenager working at Pizza Perfecto. Apparently now that summer is winding down, the kids who are gearing up for college aren't afraid to blow off a few shifts here and there for one last chance to hang out with their high school friends. Jai's not complaining. It's more money for him, right?

Pauly isn't totally happy about the situation. He's okay with the kids messing around as long as the customers get their food on time. But it pisses him off when his staff doesn't bother to turn up at all.

Well, as pissed off as Pauly ever gets.

"Aw hell, I was a kid too once," he mutters. "And not that long ago, thank you very much! I know what these idiots are like. But if I said I was gonna turn up to a job, I turned up!"

Jai's finally found something Pauly cares about.

On Wednesday Jai works a morning shift, finishes at two in the afternoon, and finds himself at a loose end. He offers to take Caden and Noah to the nearby park before dinner to give Kat a chance to unwind.

Caden is sitting on the swings. He's not swinging. Noah is attached to his legs like a sturdy little anchor, making squealing noises because he wants his big brother to pick him up and let him have a turn too. Jai is pretty sure it's going to end in tears one way or another.

Jai's distracted from the impending disaster by the unexpected arrival of Nick.

Nick looks good. He's wearing faded jeans and an even more faded T-shirt. His hair is mussed up as though he's only just crawled out of bed. He wheels his bike over to the bench where Jai is sitting, drops it on the grass, and sits down.

"Hey," Jai says.

"Hey." Nick squints at Caden and Noah and waves at them. "I, um, I swung by your house, and your scary sister said you were here."

Jai snorts. "Jesus. I'll bet you got the third degree, didn't you? She's as bad as my mom."

Nick shrugs. "It was okay."

The park is pretty empty, apart from an old woman walking a little dog along the edge of the grass. They're both moving slowly, the leash hanging limp between them. It's probably the weather, Jai figures. It's an overcast day. Not exactly perfect park weather.

"How are things with your dad?"

"Awkward." Nick's mouth quirks into something too brief to be a proper grin. More of a grimace, maybe. "Whatever, though. It's fine."

It's clearly not. Jai reaches out and curls his fingers through Nick's. "Sorry."

Nick squeezes Jai's hand a little tighter.

From over by the swings, Noah screams in outrage as Caden finally snaps and pushes him away.

"I'd better get this." Jai stands up and heads over to the boys. "Caden? You need to give Noah a turn too."

"No! I want to go high!"

"Caden. Come on, buddy."

There are three swings. One is supposed to be a baby swing, but it's broken. If Noah wants a swing, someone will have to hold him. And Noah wants a fucking swing. He's about half a minute away from total meltdown.

Caden isn't far behind. "You said you'd push me high, Uncle Jai!"

The chains on the swing set squeal as Nick sits down on the swing beside Caden's. He holds a hand down to Noah. "You can swing with me, huh, Noah?"

Noah gulps down a wail and glares suspiciously at Nick. Before Noah has time to object, Jai leans down, scoops him up, and sets him in Nick's lap. Nick holds him and uses his feet to push the swing into motion. Jai, meanwhile, gets behind Caden, grabs the seat of his swing, and draws it back as far as he can.

Caden laughs when he lets it go, and Jai sends him higher with each push.

Meanwhile, Nick and Noah swing gently beside them.

It's weirdly comfortable. Have Jai and Nick ever spent any time together and it's not been about sex? Not that they've had sex every time, but the promise of it has always been there, the anticipation. Hell, sex was the entire reason they started hanging out, whether they got to it or not. So this is all new.

Jai likes it.

He pushes Caden once more, and Caden squeals with breathless delight.

He catches Nick's gaze, and Nick looks away like he's suddenly shy.

Jai's not sure what it means, but it's nice.

Kat: *Nick came here looking for you. Did he find you?*

Kat: *I gave him directions to the park but I'm not super confident of his ability to tell left from right.*

Kat: *Why aren't you answering me?*

Kat: *You should invite Nick to dinner.*

Kat: *What's with the radio silence, little brother? Are you too busy cavorting in the park with your new boyfriend?*

Kat: *If you don't answer me, I'll start to think you've abducted my children.*

Kat: *What's wrong with me? Feel free to abduct my children anytime.*

Kat: *Should I tell Mom to set another place for dinner or not?*

"So," Jai says as they head back to the house. He's pushing Noah's stroller, and Nick is holding Caden's hand.

"So?" Nick asks.

"Do you want to stay for dinner?"

Nick flushes and ducks his head to hide a grin. "Um, okay. If it's fine with your mom and stuff."

Of course it's fine with Janice. From the moment they get back to the house and Jai mentions that he's asked Nick to stay, Janice focuses on the pair of them with the precision of a laser. Kat's not much better. And Ronny, who would usually be Jai's laid-back savior in moments like these, isn't helping much either. It's not his fault. It's because Nick keeps getting tongue-tied and calling him Mr. Green. He's also got a terrified look in his eye, like he's half-afraid Ronny can still spring a pop quiz on him.

Nick texts his parents to let them know he won't be home for dinner, and Jai notices that he doesn't wait for a response. Just slips his phone into his pocket and goes straight back to being intimidated.

"We don't stand much on ceremony here," Janice announces. "But hell, it's about time we used the dining room table instead of eating in the kitchen. Jai, go and clear the dining room table."

Jai throws her a look. He's pretty sure the dining room table hasn't been cleared since Christmas. Christmas of 1996.

"I'll help!" Nick exclaims eagerly.

The dining room table is piled high with Janice's sewing gear—*"Goddamn it! This looked so much easier on YouTube!"*—as well as a half-completed jigsaw puzzle, a teething ring, a stack of old magazines, and a tub of salon supplies.

"I think they're auditioning for the next season of *Hoarders*," Jai says.

It's easy enough to clear away most of the stuff. Jai shoves what he can into the plastic tub and sets it on the floor in the corner. He puts the sewing machine down with it, dumps the magazines next to it, then prepares to sweep the jigsaw back into the box it came from.

"No! It's half-done!" Nick exclaims. "You can't just shove it back in there. It'll break. You need to get a piece of cardboard or something, and move it onto that."

Jai heads down to the basement and comes back with a sheet of plywood. He holds it flush with the edge of the table while Nick carefully shunts the jigsaw onto it.

"My grandma used to do jigsaws," Nick tells him. "Like, all the time. She had this really cool mat you just rolled everything up into, but she never really used it. She just left the puzzle out on her table, and whoever was walking by would stop and work on it for a bit. This one Thanksgiving, it was huge—all my uncles and aunts and cousins were there—and we finished a ten-thousand-piece puzzle in three days. It was sort of cool." He catches Jai's gaze and the color rises in his cheeks. "Okay, it sounds kind of lame the way I'm telling it."

"No." Jai sets the plywood on the floor carefully. "I think I know what you mean. Sometimes it's the little things that connect us."

"Yeah." Nick smiles and fiddles with a puzzle piece. "And we used to play cards as well. She taught us how to play canasta. That's something we'd do on holidays too. Nobody watched TV after dinner. She'd get this thick green blanket out, and that was the tablecloth for cards. And everyone would sit around and play and talk for hours." He shrugs. "It was like this special thing. We only did it at Grandma's house. When we were back home, sometimes I'd ask my mom and dad if we could play, but it's not the same with only three people."

"Is this the same grandma who collected porcelain thimbles?"

"You remember that!" Nick's smile grows. "Yeah. I only really had the one grandma. I mean, I had another one, but she died before I was born, so I never even got to meet her."

"She sounds pretty amazing," Jai says.

Nick starts to sweep the stack of pieces into the box. "I guess? I mean, not to anyone else, probably. She was just a normal person who did normal stuff. Like, she never dived into a burning building to save a bunch of orphans or anything, but she was pretty amazing to me." He pauses, flipping a puzzle piece over in his hand. "At her funeral there were only six people there who weren't family. They had this guest book thing. It's probably not called a guest book. And only the first page got used. That was kind of more upsetting to me than anything."

Jai puts a hand on his shoulder.

Nick shakes his head and grins. "Wow. That all got a bit weird, didn't it? I mean my grandma was really cool is all, and just because she never walked past a burning orphanage and got the chance to prove it to the rest of the world isn't fair." His brow wrinkles in a frown. "Except for the orphans, I guess. They'd be pretty glad not to get their house burned down."

Jai isn't sure how to respond to that. Luckily Nick doesn't seem to require a response. He pushes the last of the puzzle pieces into the box, then sets it on top of the magazines.

"Nick!" Janice calls from the kitchen. "Get in here and tell me if you won't eat any of these vegetables!"

"I'll try anything, Mrs. H," Nick calls back, heading down the hall toward her.

"That's what I heard!" Kat yells, and Jai shakes his head as the kitchen erupts with laughter.

"I like your family," Nick says later, when the house is quiet and they're down in the basement, scrolling through the Netflix menu. "They're kinda rude."

"Kinda?" Jai rolls his eyes.

"I can handle your mom and your sister fine," Nick says. "But, Jai, I cannot deal with Mr. Green. Like, I know teachers are people and stuff. Just they're not the sort of people you expect to be snickering about your sex life, you know? This is very humiliating for me." His smirk belies it.

"Huh." Jai puts an arm around him. "If we're talking humiliating sex moments, have I got a story about a pool for you."

Nick elbows him. "I see your pool story, and raise you a porta-potty story."

Jai seriously considers that for a moment. "I don't know. That was bad, but your *dad*?"

Nick shudders. "You're right. The pool wins."

"I've never had a meet-the-parents moment before," Jai says. "But I'm certain that was the worst one ever."

"Yeah." Nick shakes his head. "God, that was bad."

"Sorry."

"Uh, pretty sure I started the whole skinny-dipping thing." Nick chews his bottom lip for a moment. "He'll get over it, right? Like in a decade or something?"

"Yeah. Probably."

Nick snorts and scrolls through the menu. "*Narcos* or *The X-Files*?"

"*Attack on Titan,*" Jai decides.

Nick laughs and starts the episode.

Jai wakes up feeling a little disoriented. For a moment he's not sure exactly where he is. A side-effect of never usually staying more than a few nights in one place. Then he registers the weight on his body. He's resting with his back against the arm of the couch, and Nick is sprawled on top of him, his arms around Jai's chest and his head on Jai's shoulder.

Jai's back is stiff, but not enough to move Nick.

Instead he gently cards his fingers through Nick's hair, careful not to wake him.

Attack on Titan is still playing. How many episodes has Jai missed? Who the hell are those guys in green cloaks again? Doesn't matter.

He sits there a while longer, until pressure on his bladder makes him move. He tries to slide out from under Nick without disturbing him, but it's impossible.

"Wha'?" Nick mumbles.

"Bathroom," Jai tells him quietly, then makes for the stairs.

When he gets back, Nick is awake and sitting up, although his face is creased with sleep and his hair is sticking up in odd places.

"What time is it?" Jai asks.

Nick stares at the laptop. "Not even ten."

Jai sprawls back down on the couch.

"Wanna make out for a while?" Nick asks.

Jai doesn't even have time to answer before Nick's climbing into his lap. He laughs and tilts his head to kiss Nick's throat. That always makes Nick squirm. Everything makes Nick squirm. Jai holds Nick's hips, and Nick puts his hands on Jai's shoulders.

They kiss, and Jai imagines they fit together like puzzle pieces.

"Huh," Nick says, drawing back and narrowing his eyes.

"What?"

Nick rubs his chin against Jai's cheek like an affectionate cat. "No morning breath."

"Well, it's not morning."

"No, but I thought it was more a sleep thing rather than a time-of-the-day thing." Nick kisses him again, more slowly this time, and nips at Jai's bottom lip with his teeth. "Guess not."

"It's probably the length of time you're asleep. That was hardly even a nap."

"True." Nick grinds down on Jai's thighs, his breath hot on Jai's lips as he leans in for another kiss. This one is short and teasing, barely a touch before Nick leans back again. His eyes are wide. He swallows, and his Adam's apple bobs.

"What?" Jai asks him.

Nick sucks in a breath. "Jai, can we have sex tonight?"

Jai slides a hand into the back of Nick's jeans, feeling the trail of goose bumps his touch leaves on Nick's warm skin. "Yeah. Please."

Nick shivers. "Awesome."

Jai presses his mouth to Nick's jaw. "You want to top?"

"Y-yeah." Nick shudders out a breath. His throat clicks when he swallows again. He looks half-elated, half-petrified. "Um, yeah. Awesome?"

CHAPTER TWENTY-ONE

Performance anxiety is a thing.

Nick first became aware of it when he was nine and on the local Little League team. Which turned out to involve more than squatting in the dugout, trying to catch insects, or standing in the outfield, pretending he was Ben 10. Like there were games with scores and everything. And expectations. And, after the great chickenpox debacle of 2006, when half the team was struck down, suddenly Nick had been expected to step up and not just warm the bench. He'd actually been put third on the batting roster. Things had been *that* serious. For the entire week preceding the game, Nick had quietly panicked that he would mess it up. His mom and dad were coming to the game and *everything*.

If Nick's life had been something from the Disney Channel, he totally would have hit a home run that day. Knocked it right out of the park. There would have been wild cheering and lots of slow motion. And probably a humorously humiliated villain. Instead Nick had been so overcome with nerves that his performance anxiety had ratcheted straight up into nightmarish stage fright, and he'd dropped his bat and vomited all over home base.

It's a thing.

But Nick's an adult now, right? He is *not* going to vomit on home base this time.

Home base being Jai's ass.

He is stupidly nervous. Like, they've had sex before, but when Nick was bottoming, it wasn't like he had to do much but let Jai take charge, right? And now Nick kind of has to lead. He wishes he'd watched more porn. And actually paid attention to the technique, instead of just jerking off furiously and collapsing in a boneless, sticky heap on his mattress.

Okay.

Okay, yeah, he's got this.

They make out for a little while, and Nick tries to concentrate on the pressure of Jai's lips, and the scrape of his stubble, and that cool thing he does with his tongue, and not worry about where it's going. All he has to do is concentrate on this moment, and let the heat and the friction build between them.

And it's *good*. It's so good. Kissing Jai is definitely on the list of Nick's favorite things. It's like floating in the pool in the middle of a hot night, tiny laps of cool sensation playing over his skin. His fingers scrabble at the back of Jai's T-shirt, and Jai breaks their kiss and leans back for a moment so he can pull the shirt off.

Nick loves the way Jai's muscles bunch and shift under his skin.

It's amazing. Human beings are amazing. Like how muscles and sinew and bones and blood all make up this ridiculously complicated apparatus that somehow works, and moves, and thinks, and kisses. Electrical impulses translate into action and emotion. It's miraculous.

Also, Nick should have paid more attention in biology.

Also also, it's totally not a surprise that the closest thing he's ever had to a religious experience involves Jai Hazenbrook taking his shirt off.

Nick hides his grin in the curve of Jai's shoulder, and presses his mouth to Jai's warm skin.

He shivers as Jai's hands slide under his shirt, his fingers following the line of Nick's spine. He's so hard right now. He rocks forward, seeking contact, friction, and Jai slips one hand down the back of his jeans.

Fuck.

Nick leans back. "Um, we should unfold the couch?"

Jai looks dazed, his lips kiss-bitten. "Yeah."

Nick slides off his lap, and stands on legs that he's not entirely sure will hold him.

The couch screeches and groans as they pull it out into a bed. The legs scrape against the thin carpet. Then Jai fetches the condoms and lube, and tosses them onto the bed. Nick picks them up, his heart thumping as he toes his sneakers off.

Jai pops the button on his fly. "You okay with this?"

Nick lets out a shaky breath. "Pretty sure I'm gonna screw it up."

Jai regards him curiously for a moment. "How are you gonna screw it up, Nick?"

"Um, like, coming the second I even get near your ass?"

Jai shrugs and flashes him an easy grin. "So? Then we can either call it a night, or just mess around until you're ready to go again. Whatever works."

Nick huffs out something close to a laugh and sets the condoms and lube back down on the end of the thin mattress. "It's that simple, huh?"

"Yep," Jai says, and tugs down his zipper. "It's that simple."

Then he shoves his jeans down, and Nick is momentarily deafened by an angelic choir.

Jai's dick.

There are not enough superlatives in the world to describe Jai's dick. It's a thing of beauty, and Nick's mouth waters at the sight of it. It's just perfect, okay? It's a perfect length and a perfect girth, and even the veins aren't too weird and veiny. It also doesn't hurt that Nick already knows how good it feels in his mouth and his ass.

He regards Jai's dick somewhat regretfully.

Sorry, buddy, but you don't get a starring role tonight.

He'll make things up to it later.

Repeatedly, hopefully.

Nick fumbles with his own jeans and underwear, and then, when he's finally free of them, he realizes he's still wearing his socks. Not cool. He bends over to tug them off. When he straightens up again, Jai's sitting down. The springs wheeze and sigh.

"How do you want me?" Jai asks him.

"Um, however you'll be most comfortable?" Nick asks, secretly impressed with how he doesn't even stammer.

Jai stretches out on the bed on his stomach. He rests his cheek on his folded arms like he's waiting for a massage. Which he kind of is? Nick picks up the lube, his heart hammering.

Shit shit shit.

But also, holy fuck *yes*.

Nick's gaze travels up Jai's naked body and hits a roadblock at the back of his left hip.

He laughs. "Found it!"

Jai's tattoo. It's a stylized tree. Okay, Nick was not expecting a tree. It's probably the tree of life or something, right? Or that tree that Buddha meditated under until he found enlightenment. Something representing Jai's interconnectedness with the universe and stuff.

He climbs onto the bed and presses his fingers gently against the tattoo.

"My dad used to take me fishing," Jai says. "We always sat under the same tree. When I left Franklin, I wasn't leaving that, you know? I needed to take that with me."

Nick leans over him and presses a kiss to his shoulder. "I like it. It's nice."

He runs his hand down Jai's back, and Jai lets out a slow breath.

Okay, yeah. Nick can do this. He only fumbles the lube once, and doesn't even laugh when it makes a farting sound as he squeezes some onto his fingers. Maturity, FTW.

Jai shifts his legs apart.

His ass is . . . Nick kind of wants to bite it. Like, a lot. And maybe growl while he does it? Instead he settles for stroking it with his dry hand, and feeling the muscles jump under his palm.

Okay, yeah.

Okay.

Nick's heart is racing. He slides his lubed fingers into the cleft of Jai's ass, trying to remember how it felt when Jai did this to him. Except he can't even remember his own name right now. He presses a fingertip against Jai's hole. Jai shifts again, and Nick pushes in just a fraction. It's tight and hot, but not as weird as Nick thought it would be. He has a finger in another guy's ass. But also, awesome!

He works his finger in slowly. "Is that okay?"

"Yeah." Jai moves like he can't quite get comfortable, and it takes Nick a second to realize he's rubbing himself against the mattress. Like he's getting into it. He likes what Nick's doing, but it's not enough. That realization hits with a jolt, and Nick feels breathless and powerful all at the same time.

Nick removes his finger carefully, then slides two inside. Because sex, really, is just another form of exercise, right? It's all about the stretching. First with his fingers, and then . . .

No. Nick is not even going to think about putting his dick inside Jai yet, or he'll blow. In fact, Nick is going to completely forget that he even has a dick, and just concentrate on what his fingers are doing to Jai's body. He'll study and catalog every little reaction, like this is a science experiment or something, and not the hottest guy in the universe trying to come apart on his fingers.

Nick's not actually sure how he gets through the next few minutes. Or decades. Or maybe eons. It's entirely possible he slips into a fugue state as a coping mechanism. That seems like something he would do. Whenever the going gets tough, his rational brain detaches like an escape pod and spins off into space.

"Okay," Jai murmurs, his breath rasping. "Now, Nick. I'm ready."

Jai gets his knees under him.

Shit shit shit.

Nick fumbles with the condoms. He tears the first one open, and then puts his thumb through it. The second one he manages to roll on without coming at his own touch, so yay for him. Still, he tightens his thumb and forefinger around the base of his dick to make sure, and gets into position.

Where are his knees supposed to go, exactly?

Oh, okay. No, this sort of makes sense. Yeah, he can totally line his dick up with Jai's ass like this. And . . . and right now would be the time to start thinking of baseball stats. Or, because he hates baseball, right now would be the time to start running through the members of Rogue Squadron.

Oh wow. Holy fuck! Jai's ass is opening for his dick, and this is fucking *incredible.*

Rogue Leader, go!

Nick has to squeeze his eyes shut when he bottoms out. He lays a shaking hand on Jai's hip, and curls his fingers around it. Because if he doesn't hang on to something, he's going to shatter into a million pieces. Because it's so tight, so hot, and Nick has never felt pressure like this on his dick before. If it wasn't so fucking excruciating trying to hold himself together, he'd probably ask Jai if he could live in his ass.

"Okay?" Jai asks.

"Y-yeah. Just trying to, um . . ." To not come like a geyser.

"Feels good, Nick." Jai groans. "So good."

That is probably a lie, but Nick will take the ego boost. He pulls back, then thrusts slowly forward again. Jai has a prostate he should he aiming for, right? Nick will totally get on that as soon as he gets this motion thing sorted out. Because two—three now—awkward thrusts do not a rhythm make.

What if Jai's prostate is like the thermal exhaust point on the first Death Star? How is Nick supposed to find it? He's not Luke Skywalker. He's never bull's-eyed womp rats in his T-16 back home.

And okay, he should probably stop thinking about Star Wars now.

Three strokes become four, become five, but six is apparently out of the question, because suddenly Nick's coming, fingers tightening on Jai's hips, body shuddering, and all the coiled tension in his balls letting go just like that.

"Fuck." Nick half collapses over Jai, gasping. Tremors run through him like the aftershocks of some massive quake.

Okay, so that was embarrassingly fast, but not as embarrassingly fast as it could have been. It's not much of a distinction, but Nick's going to hold on to it.

He pulls out of Jai and stumbles over toward the trash can in the corner to dispose of the condom. And to maybe take a moment to think about how to apologize? When he turns around again, Jai's lying on his back, legs wide, tugging on his dick like it isn't even a little bit weird to do that in front of someone. Which of course it isn't, considering Nick just had his dick in Jai's ass, right?

Jai's gaze is fixed on Nick like he's something worth looking at, even though Nick is sweaty and bright red.

Jai strokes himself off with his left hand. He cups his balls with his right hand, squeezes, then moves his hand lower and shoves two fingers inside his ass. His abs tighten, his body jackknifes, and then he's coming all over his stomach and chest.

It's probably the hottest thing Nick has ever seen.

"Holy shit," Nick whispers, and Jai gives him a lazy smile.

Nick pads to the laundry tub, finds a washcloth, wets it, and heads back over to Jai.

"That was, um . . ."

"It was good, Nick." Jai takes the cloth and wipes the spunk off his stomach, then the lube off his ass and inner thighs.

Nick lies down beside him. "I'll probably be better at it next time."

"We both came," Jai says. "I'm not complaining."

"Fuck, me neither. Just, um, you know how you said to watch porn with twinks plowing bigger guys?"

"Yeah."

"Well, maybe next time I want to plow the fuck out of you. Like hard-core piston action, you know?"

Jai grins. "That sounds like something I'd be into, sure."

Nick wonders if Jai knows how cool he is. About everything, and not just Nick being not very good at sex. *Yet.* Because Nick is going to practice, and, one day soon, he's going to add Jai's mind to the list of things he can blow, and it's going to be incredible.

Nick tries to think about that, without thinking about the countdown timer running in the back of his head, telling him summer's almost over. Telling him *this* is almost over. Because he knew the deal from the start. Other things may have changed, but that hasn't.

At the end of the summer, he'll have to say good-bye.

It's probably going to hurt.

Nick: *I think I have feelings.*

Devon: *Called it, bro.*

Nick: *WHAT?*

Devon: *Jai's a cool guy and you're a marshmallow. This was sort of inevitable?*

Nick: *Maybe I wasn't even talking about Jai, asshole.*

Devon: *Who were u talking about, then?*

Nick: *Fuck you.*

Devon: *Called it.*

Devon: *U still there?*

Devon: *Do u want me to come over?*

Devon: *I'm coming over to snuggle the fuck out of u, Nick.*

Devon: *If u don't answer me, I'll know u want me to come over.*

Devon: *Nick? R u seriously pissed at me?*
Devon: *Seriously?*
Devon: *Meatlovers or Hawaiian?*
Nick: *Meatlovers.*

CHAPTER TWENTY-TWO

Jai wakes up to the sounds of someone rattling around in the kitchen upstairs. He yawns and stretches and scratches his belly. He waits until he can no longer ignore his bladder, then rolls out of bed and heads for the bathroom. When he's finished in the bathroom, he steps into the hallway to find Caden dancing from foot to foot desperately.

"I really need to peeeeee!" he exclaims, diving under Jai's arm to get through the door.

When Jai enters the kitchen, Noah is sitting naked on the floor, wearing a plastic colander on his head. Janice is making pancakes, Ronny is fighting with the coffee machine, and Kat is sitting at the table, reading something on her phone.

"You know what?" Janice asks. "Screw this. We should go to Denny's instead. Your dad always used to take us to Denny's at least once a week. Remember that, kids?"

"Uh-huh," Jai says. "Until he went on his health kick."

"And we all know how *that* ended," Janice mutters, furiously stirring the pancake batter.

Kat stares at Jai, openmouthed, and he stares back.

"What?" Janice asks, sticking her finger in the batter to taste it. "I'm just saying he might as well have worn an ass-groove into the couch and stuffed his face with potato chips every day for all the difference it made."

It's a fair point, Jai guesses.

"Jeez, Mom," Kat says.

"What?" Janice asks again.

Ronny snorts, and then whoops when the coffee machine hisses and spits and coffee starts to burble out of it. "Oh yeah!"

Caden bounces into the kitchen. "Are we having pancakes?"

"Yep," Janice says. "As soon as I can find the goddamn pan."

"It's in the drainer," Kat tells her.

"Jai?" Ronny holds up a coffee mug.

"Thanks, yeah."

"Did Nick stay over?" Janice asks.

Jai frowns. "No."

"Don't get all defensive. I was just wondering how many I'm making breakfast for."

"I wasn't being defensive!"

"You are now," Janice points out, and wrestles the pan onto the stovetop.

Jai opens his mouth to retaliate, then shuts it again. It's his mom. He can't win this thing.

Ronny hands him his mug of coffee.

"Nick probably needs to be up early to go to daycare," Kat suggests, an evil grin twitching around the corners of her mouth.

"This shit again?" Jai asks, bristling. "Seriously?"

"Oh, it never gets old," Kat tells him. "And neither does Nick!"

Ronny high-fives her.

Jai takes his coffee and stalks into the living room.

"Jai?" Kat calls after him. "I was only kidding, asshole!"

Jai ignores her and slumps onto the sofa. Fuck it. He'll drink his coffee, and then he's going to grab a shower and get dressed and go to McDonald's for breakfast, and he's going to eat something disgusting and full of grease and plastic cheese.

"Jai," Ronny says, sitting down in the easy chair opposite the sofa. "You know we're only playing, right? You don't usually bite so easily."

"Yeah, I don't really want to talk about this, okay?"

"Sure, man." Ronny gives him a shrewd look. "That because it's hitting too close to home or something?"

"He's eighteen," Jai mutters.

"Yeah, but he's a young eighteen," Ronny says.

"You're gonna start on me too?"

"No. I'm just saying Nick's a kid who's got a lot of growing up to do. It's not a bad thing, but it's true." Ronny shakes his head and smiles. "Like, these kids. They spend an hour a day in your class, and they somehow think they're invisible. Like you don't notice a damn thing about them. Who they're dating, and what drama they're going through this week, and when their friends shit on them, or they shit on their friends. They really think that teachers have no idea what's going on in their lives. But we notice."

Jai remembers when he was in school, thinking that the teachers somehow didn't exist beyond the vacuum of the classroom. That they weren't people with their own lives in the outside world. He wonders what any of them had been thinking when they looked at him: an angry, defiant, ultimately naive kid who'd been desperate to get out of town, so sure that all the answers to his indistinct dreams were just over the horizon. Jai's older now, tempered by experience. He hopes he's a little wiser too.

He quirks his mouth in a wry smile and meets Ronny's gaze. "And what'd you notice about Nick?"

"Oh, where do I even start?" Ronny snorts. "Smart, but scatterbrained. Can't concentrate on a task to save his life. Mostly happy. Loyal to his friends. And looking for his place still. A typical eighteen-year-old kid."

Jai nods.

"Obsessed with Tolkien. And some really weird anime." Ronny's smile grows. "Geeky, very geeky, but self-aware enough to get away with it. Smarter than he lets on, because he's not confident enough to draw that kind of target on his back when he's already out as a gay kid in a small town. Ridiculously codependent with Devon."

Jai takes a sip of his coffee. "Yeah, I already know that one."

"I mean, seriously, this one day Devon was sick, and by the look on Nick's face, you would have thought someone had drowned his puppy in front of him. But also, Nick's genuinely a decent kid. And that's kind of a rare thing. Teenagers can be assholes to each other." Ronny shrugs. "But yeah, he's got a lot of growing up to do still."

Jai grunts.

"Your mom is right. You really are defensive about him, you know?" Ronny raises his eyebrows. "He's a good kid is what I'm saying. Hey, if you can put up with the stream of consciousness and pop culture references he cobbles together and considers a language, good for you. You could do a lot worse. And so could he."

Jai thinks about that for a moment. "It's just a short-term thing, though, until he goes to college and meets someone else."

"You sure he's gonna meet someone else?"

"Isn't that what college is all about?"

"As a trained educator, I feel I should stress that college is about higher learning, but you're right." Ronny laughs. "It's about getting away from home and hooking up with a bunch of different people."

Jai smiles and ignores the twist in his gut when he thinks of Nick doing exactly that.

Ronny shrugs. "Nick's more shy than he comes across though. He doesn't put himself out there, you know? Maybe that's from being the little gay kid in a small town, but he hasn't got as much self-confidence as he tries to project. He's a loud, annoying little shit when he's playing Devon's sidekick, but on his own, he's . . ." He shrugs again. "I think he's gonna have a hard time in college by himself."

"I assumed he and Devon would be attached at the hip until death," Jai says.

"Different colleges. Gonna be rough on both of them."

Jai wonders if that's really true. Nick hasn't talked much about college, beyond not knowing if it's what he wants to do, and he certainly hasn't talked about going to college without Devon. So maybe it's not as big a deal as Ronny seems to think it is. Of course, the fact he hasn't talked about it could mean the exact opposite: that he's scared. Jai feels an unpleasant jolt in his stomach. It makes a lot of sense. Nick is scared of his future. It's not like he spelled it out that night in Devon's room, but he was drunk enough to come damn close. Jai wonders why Nick doesn't just admit it straight-out. Maybe he thinks Jai wouldn't get it. Maybe he thinks Jai would think less of him. Or maybe he thinks they're just not in the sort of relationship where they can talk about things like that.

How the hell would either of them know, unless they try?

Nick: *Would it be weird if I invited u on a date?*
Jai: *It would certainly be different.*
Nick: *Except I don't have any money and nor do u.*
Jai: *Yes, that is a problem.*

Nick: *I don't think my dad would let me break into my college savings just so I could take you someplace there is lobster.*

Jai: *Probably not.*

Nick: *Do u even like lobster?*

Jai: *It's ok.*

Nick: *What if I bought a tin of lobster meat from the store and then we mixed it in ramen or something?*

Jai: *That sounds disgusting.*

Nick: *Just the ramen, then?*

Jai: *I like ramen.*

Nick: *My dad is making hot dogs on the grill tonight.*

Nick: *It's this thing where he fries them.*

Nick: *It sounds gross, but it's actually really nice.*

Nick: *What do u think?*

Jai: *What do I think of fried hot dogs?*

Nick: *Fuck. I was supposed to invite u over in the middle of all that. Wanna come to my place tonight for a swim and then some hot dogs?*

Jai: *Okay. Should I bring wine or beer for your parents?*

Nick: *Um . . .*

Jai: *Do they know I'm 25 and can legally buy alcohol?*

Nick: *Maybe just bring some soda?*

Chris Stahlnecker nods at Jai when he arrives at Nick's house. There's no handshake. There's also no acknowledgment that the first time he met Jai, Jai was halfway to violating his naked teenage son in his pool, so Jai's going to count the no-handshake thing as a win.

"Hey, Jai!" Nick bounces down the stairs. "Um, you remember my dad, right?"

Until the day he dies.

Chris's eye twitches.

"Oh, um, yeah, so we're gonna just get in the pool or whatever," Nick says, flushing.

Chris lands them both with a withering glare.

"Just, um, for a swim," Nick clarifies, rubbing the back of his neck. "Come on, Jai."

The water is cool. Jai and Nick sit on the pool step for a moment, and then Jai slides into the deeper water. He can't shake the feeling that Chris Stahlnecker is standing just behind the kitchen windows, glaring out at him.

The afternoon softens slowly into evening.

The noises of the neighborhood settle over Jai like music he remembers from childhood summers that seem so long ago now. He hears a dog barking a few houses down. In the other direction, little kids are shrieking with laughter to the rhythmic squeak and thump of a trampoline. Cars on the street. Doors opening and closing. A phone ringing. The faint strains of someone's stereo drifting over the back fence. A mom yells for her kids to get inside and wash their hands, and she sounds like she could be a million miles away.

Jai lazes in the water while Nick shoots him quick, shy smiles.

He can smell someone cooking dinner nearby.

A few yards away, someone starts up a lawn mower.

The sounds and smells of a dying day, of a dying summer. Jai lets them lap at him as gently as the water.

Hard to imagine that to someone else, this suburban small-town life could be as foreign and magical as a Vietnamese temple, or a Bavarian castle, or the wide, empty expanse of the Nullarbor.

It's peaceful.

Until Nick flicks water in his face and laughs.

"What?" Jai asks, a grin tugging at his mouth.

"Nothin'." Nick slicks his wet hair back, and it immediately stands up again like the crest of a parrot. "I just wanted to mess with you."

"Consider me messed with."

Nick's smile is somehow softer than those Jai is used to seeing from him. "Thanks for coming over. I wasn't sure you would, because, you know, my *parents*."

Jai reaches out and tangles his wet fingers with Nick's. "We're boyfriends, right? This is what boyfriends do?"

"I guess." Nick wrinkles his nose. "I haven't had a boyfriend before."

"Me neither."

"Really? Oh *please*, as if I believe that!"

"Really."

"Oh." Nick flushes and is silent for a moment. He looks down, and water drips off the end of his nose. When he looks up again, he's smiling. "That's very cool."

Jai gazes at him. His boyfriend. His first boyfriend. And yeah, it is very cool. He's never sought out relationships before, and never felt the need. He's never thought he was missing out on anything. But now that he's accidentally stumbled into a relationship, he likes it. Nick shows parts of himself that he wouldn't if they'd only known each other for a few days, or a single night, those short-lived but intense encounters that are all Jai has to compare *this* to. Every moment with Nick, however prosaic, is another moment of discovery. Every conversation, however mundane, is also part revelation.

He remembers getting lost once in the Czech Republic. Stepping off a train in the wrong town, with no idea where he was or where to find his way to where he was supposed to be. He'd never even heard of Loket before he'd stumbled across it. Everything had been unplanned for, unexpected. Everything had been an adventure. Every discovery a treasure.

Nick Stahlnecker is Loket.

When it gets dark, Chris comes outside and cooks hot dogs on the grill. Marnie brings out a bowl of salad and a potato casserole.

Jai would rather not get out of the pool, actually, but he gives Nick a smile that shows a lot more confidence than he actually feels, wraps himself in a towel, and sits down at the picnic table on the back patio for what he expects will be an interrogation.

It's actually not as bad as he thinks.

It's not great, but it's not the Spanish Inquisition.

Chris manages to give him a lecture about how he should be saving for the future, and putting the money he earns into investments rather than "throwing it all away." And Marnie worries that his mother must worry. Does she worry? Oh, but she must. And Jai really doesn't know how to respond to that. Does Janice worry about him? Probably, sure, the same way she still worries about Kat. The same way that they worry about her. Like family. Not like . . . like whatever the hell it is when Marnie reaches over and pets Nick on the head, and he tries to duck away, face burning, and can't meet Jai's gaze for a long time afterward.

"Sorry about them," Nick mutters later, when he and Jai are loading the dishwasher in the kitchen.

"It wasn't so bad," Jai says.

Nick scowls and scrapes down a plate over the sink. "Um, yeah, it was. But thanks."

He scrubs furiously at the plate.

"Hey." Jai puts a hand on his shoulder, and he's not entirely surprised when Nick sets the plate down and turns into his embrace. He rubs his hands down Nick's spine.

"They treat me like a kid," Nick says in a quiet voice. "Which, well, okay, because what other option have I ever given them? But now it's like we're all stuck in this holding pattern and nobody knows what to do."

Jai doesn't fully understand that. His family shattered the day his dad died. Everything was different after that. Everything changed, especially Jai's relationship with his mom. She wasn't indestructible, and he couldn't see her that way anymore. Not when he'd picked her up off the floor so many times. Not when she'd done the same to him when it was his turn to break. They hadn't had a holding pattern. They'd had a fucking midair collision. Flaming wreckage and bodies everywhere, but they got through it. They worked it out together.

"It's okay. You'll figure this out, you know?"

Nick nods and sniffles. "Fuck, I'm an idiot."

"Nah." Jai pats him on the back. He's aware of someone standing in the hallway outside the kitchen door, but by the time he looks up, whoever it was is gone. "You're just a scruffy nerf herder."

"Pretty sure that's not a compliment!" But Nick laughs anyway, and turns back to the sink.

Jai loads the plates into the dishwasher as Nick hands them to him.

When Jai finally makes it home, there's a package waiting for him on the kitchen table.

It's his new backpack.

Nick: *So my parents don't totally hate u.*
Jai: *Probably the best I could hope for.*
Nick: *Probably! :D*
Jai: *It was worth it for the hot dogs.*
Nick: *They're good, right?*
Jai: *Really good.*
Nick: *Are u working tomorrow?*
Jai: *Noon until 8.*
Nick: *Cool. Can we hang after?*
Jai: *I'd love that.*
Nick. *:D*

CHAPTER ✦ TWENTY-THREE

Nick has always hated the end of summer. He hates the way the days yellow at the edges like the pages of an old book. He hates the way the heat stops soaking into his bones and lies on the surface of his skin instead, the first hint that the season is turning. In the past, Nick has always marked the end of summer, and mourned it, by the subtle changes in the world around him, but this year he won't even have that. By the time the air cools and the days shorten, he'll be at college. This year the end of summer won't just mean a loss of freedom, it will mean the loss of his childhood.

Nick ekes out every last minute with a growing sense of desperation.

He hangs out at Pizza Perfecto, or in the pool, or in Jai's basement. When he's not there, he bounces between his house and Devon's, bike tires spinning on the dusty road between them like they have every summer since he was a kid, eating up the miles, eating up the moments.

He's not sure why he's still riding his bike. His dad folded and gave him back the car. Maybe Nick just wants to feel like a kid for as long as he can.

He tries to tell himself it's been a good summer, and that he's ready for whatever comes next.

At least he's not going to be a virgin at college, right? So, yeah, the entire college situation still makes him feel sick to his stomach when he thinks about it—so he doesn't think about it. He also doesn't think about how he's going to miss Jai when he's at college and Jai is in Argentina.

It was just a short-term thing, anyway. No strings and all that. And hey, how much does Nick rock at this whole boyfriend situation? They've never even had an actual fight. And the sex is awesome. Jai is totally going to be that guy whom all the other guys in Nick's life will never be able to live up to. He shall exist as perfection in Nick's memory, with a corona of light radiating around him like a smug Byzantine saint. All Nick has to do is get past Jai and make it to those other guys, right? He needs to accept Jai is just another thing that's going to fade at the end of summer. Circle of life and all that shit.

"Nick? Are you even listening to me?"

Nick starts. "What? Yes. Totally."

Devon snorts and flops back down onto his bed beside Nick. "Liar."

Nick jabs him in the ribs.

Devon jerks away from him. "Fucker!"

The mattress bounces a little, and they jostle against one another. Nick turns his face toward Devon's window so he doesn't have to look at the stack of boxes beside Devon's desk, and the empty duffel bags slung on top of them.

He grabs Devon's pillow. "Ugh."

"Ugh what?" Devon asks.

"Just everything." Nick jams the pillow in his face. It smells like Devon's body spray and some sort of weird shampoo. Like apples or something? Since when has Devon used apple-scented shampoo? Oh, that's probably Ebony. Is it weird that Nick is secondhand smelling his best friend's girlfriend's hair? That's probably weird. Nick sniffs one more time and tosses the pillow aside. "Everything."

Devon doesn't say anything else. He just does what he's always done: he pulls Nick into a hug.

It's weird that more people don't cuddle. Like usually it's a little kid thing or, if it's adults, it's a significant-other thing. Nick's not sure why that is. Who made that a rule? Why is any close contact over a few seconds suddenly laden with meaning? Cuddling is the greatest thing in the world. It doesn't have to be weird. Although he supposes it's not entirely innocent. If it were Jai cuddling him instead of Devon, Nick would already have his hands down his jeans. Down both their jeans, probably. But if cuddling is all that's on offer, then Nick will happily accept.

"The last person I cuddled with on your bed was Jai," Nick mumbles into Devon's neck.

Devon snorts. "Don't kill the moment, bro."

Nick grins, but his stomach twists too.

Because yeah, all they have left now are moments.

Nick: *:D R u working tonight?*
Jai: *Sorry, yeah. Catch up tomorrow night?*
Nick: *K!*

Seeing Devon's boxes and bags sitting by his desk waiting to get packed is bad enough, but when Nick gets home, he finds all his clothes laid out in serried lines on the floor in front of his closet. His mom is standing there, notebook in hand and a pen protruding from her pursed lips like a lady's elegant cigarette holder in a black-and-white film.

"Mom!" Nick's stab of fear shrinks in the face of his righteous indignation. "You can't just go through my closet!"

Marnie looks surprised, and Nick really, really doesn't want to have to explain. His mom can't be that naive, surely. She was a teenager once. With urges and whatnot. Except Nick doesn't really want to think about his mom's whatnot, so he huffs out an outraged breath and thanks Baby Jeebus that all his porn is stored on his laptop. And that he no longer has a stash of weed tucked in a shoebox on the top shelf of his closet. He's pretty sure he smoked the last of that before his SAT, half because he thought it would be funny, and half to blunt the edges of his rising panic. Probably more the second one, if Nick is honest. But since when is Nick honest?

"God!" Nick reaches down and plucks a T-shirt off the top of the stack, just because he can. He wrenches his dresser drawer open and shoves the shirt inside. "Do we seriously have to do this *now*?"

"What are you talking about, Nick?" It's the look of honest-to-God confusion on her face that really pisses him off. Because he's tried, hasn't he? He's tried to broach this with her, and with his dad, but they just don't hear him. It feels like he's trapped underwater, struggling, drowning, but whenever he gets the attention of the people on the surface by waving his arms, they just smile and wave back.

Nick slams the drawer shut with his knee. "*This*! You're always on my case about packing and clothes and college! Why can't you give me a fucking break for once?"

His mom jerks back as though he's slapped her.

Nick's an asshole, he knows, for taking this tone with his mom. It's just . . . It's easier to yell at her than it is to yell at his dad. It's not fair on her, but it's easier.

"Nick? What's the matter with you?" Her tone is uncertain this time.

He's an asshole. He's such a fucking asshole.

He grabs his phone off his desk. "I'm going out."

Nick is halfway down the stairs before his mom recovers her equilibrium.

"Nick?" she calls.

Nick dives into the sunlight, slamming the front door shut behind him. He picks up his bike from around the side of the garage, and races off down the road.

He doesn't even know where he's going.

Story of his fucking life.

Dad: *Where are you?*

There's a little gully at the end of a dead-end street a few houses away from Nick's. He and Devon used to play here when they were kids, because hello, it's a gully, full of dirt and insects, except after rain, when it's full of mud and insects. When they were eleven, it was kind of perfect. For fighting Sand People on Tatooine. For finding pirate treasure. For experimenting with cherry bombs and, later, with cigarettes and weed.

It's kind of a dump, actually. It's full of broken glass and trash, and probably snakes as well. Actually, this might have been why their parents disapproved. Not because they were the fun police, but because they didn't want their sons to get rabies, tetanus, or abducted by villainous hobos from black-and-white movies.

Nick dumps his bike in the grass and slides into the gully.

A part of him wants to look past the glass, dead clumps of grass, and broken bits of plywood with *fuck* and *cock* sprayed on them, and see something of the magical land that he and Devon built here once in their imaginations. Another part of him knows that he never can, that if he wanted to keep that fantasy alive, he shouldn't have come here.

Except he couldn't think of anywhere else to go.

He buries his head in his knees and cries.

Devon: *Are you okay?*
Nick: *Yeah. Just same old.*
Devon: *Call your mom, bro. She's freaking out.*

When Nick was eight, he ran away from home. Something to do with not being allowed to dress up as Frodo. Because he'd managed to score an invite to a popular kid's birthday party—he thinks his mom knew her mom—and it was a themed party. It was pirates and princesses, and, well, fuck that. Why couldn't it be pirates and princesses and hobbits? So after having a tantrum when his mom brought home his pirate costume, Nick had decided to run away. Because *then* they'd feel sorry they were ever mean to him, right?

He'd made it as far as the convenience store five blocks from home, where he'd spent all his money on Red Vines, had major buyer's remorse *and* a panic attack, and the man behind the counter had called his mom to come and collect him.

His mom didn't make him go to the party after that.

Nick still isn't sure of the lesson he learned that day.

He didn't get to be Frodo. He didn't end up going to the party at all.

Maybe there wasn't a lesson. Maybe there never is.

Jai: *Your dad called me.*
Nick: *WHAT?!?!?!?*
Jai: *I think he got my number from Devon. He's worried about you.*
Nick: *Ugh.*
Jai: *Where are you?*
Nick: *Can I come to ur place?*
Jai: *Ok.*

Jai is ridiculously cool about it when Nick turns up on his doorstep, covered in sweat and pretty much still a crying mess. It doesn't matter, Nick supposes, because this thing between them has almost run its course, so who cares if Jai sees him like this? He never had much dignity to hold on to anyway, did he?

Jai gets him a glass of water and then leads him down into the basement. *Attack on Titan* is already queued up and ready to go. Jai doesn't say anything. Just sits down with him on the couch, holds his hand, and starts the episode.

Like he knows this is exactly what Nick needs right now. Not questions, not words, just this.

Nick is in love with Jai Hazenbrook.

He's not dumb enough to say that though. He sits with Jai and sips his water, and they watch the episode in silence. When the closing credits start playing, Nick sets his glass down on the coffee table, takes a deep breath, and says, "So, I kind of yelled at my mom like an asshole today."

Jai nods, and still doesn't say anything.

"I don't want to go to college." Nick feels something inside him break like a dam wall in a disaster movie when the pressure behind it gets to be too much, and suddenly the words are flooding out of him.

"I'm scared, and it's dumb to be scared, but I am, and I know I'm going to fuck up. I'll be one of those kids you hear about who has no friends, and nobody knows who they are, but the other kids totally get a pass on their exams because some loser in their class slit his own wrists or whatever!"

Jai's eyes widen. "Nick. Jesus!"

Nick groans. "No . . . I don't mean that. I mean, I don't *think* I mean that. I don't know! I don't know what I want to do, and I don't know how to be what they want me to be, and I know I just sound like some whiny emo brat or something, but all of this stuff, I won't be able to handle it. I'm *not* handling it."

"Okay," Jai says, and he sounds so calm, and not at all like his boyfriend just word vomited all over him and threw in some bonus suicidal ideation. He takes Nick's hand and squeezes it. "You don't have to have everything figured out. You don't have to have *anything* figured out. It really is okay."

"It's not though," Nick mumbles.

Jai squeezes his hand tighter. His gaze is kind of intense. "No, it is. We're gonna make sure that it is."

"How?" Nick asks, and hates the way he sounds like a little kid.

Also, how is it possible that Jai is only seven years older than him but it's like he has all the answers? Or at least like the questions don't make him want to curl up in a corner and cry? How is that possible?

Jai leans in and presses his lips against Nick's gently. "That's the part we're going to figure out together."

Devon: *R u okay?*
Nick: *Yeah.*
Devon: *R u home?*
Nick: *Dad came and got me from Jai's place.*
Devon: *Did u talk to him?*
Nick: *I guess. Kind of.*
Devon: *U need to talk to ur dad. U need to tell him what you're feeling.*
Nick: *What if I don't know what I'm feeling?*

Devon: *U remember in 3rd grade when we had to do those book reports and rate them on a scale of smiley face to frowny face?*

Nick: *You think I should just draw my dad a frowny face?*

Devon: *I'm trying to think outside the box here.*

Nick: *You are an idiot. ILY but u are an idiot. Also, don't think I don't know it was u on the phone to my mom tonight.*

Devon: *Because if u won't tell them how bad it is, that's when I step up, bro.*

Nick: *I TRIED TO TELL THEM!*

Devon: *Ok, but maybe you think you tried, when maybe instead you were deflecting and going off on tangents and shit like always?*

Nick: *Don't*

Devon: *Nick, ILY, but u have a massive blind spot when it comes to some stuff.*

Nick: *Fuck you.*

Devon: *Ok. I can deal with u being angry at me for going behind ur back. But I'm not sorry for talking to ur mom.*

Nick: *I am so done with this conversation right now. Fuck you.*

Devon: *I love you.*

Nick: *Don't.*

Devon: *I'll talk to u later.*

Nick: *No.*

CHAPTER  TWENTY-FOUR

Every year, two weeks before the kids head off to college, Pauly throws a party at Pizza Perfecto. He closes the store at 8 p.m. on a Wednesday night, and lets the kids basically run riot through the place.

Ebony is sitting cross-legged on the front counter.

Tyler is making streamers out of toilet paper.

Two kids are making out in one of the booths.

There's a keg in the kitchen.

The breadsticks and olives have been broken out, and a very messy baseball match is underway.

It's chaotic.

"Jesus," Jai says when an olive misses his head by inches. "This place is a fucking mess!"

"I don't care," Pauly says with a grin and shrugs. "One night a year I pay for a keg, and for cleaners to come in tomorrow and pretty much douse this place in bleach, but you know what? These kids come back and work for me every vacation. They get their little brothers and sisters to apply for jobs here."

Jai snorts.

"What?" Pauly asks. "You telling me that next summer you won't be back here asking for work? You really wanna go back to construction?"

"I'm not gonna lie, Pauly. The money's a lot better in construction."

"Sure," Pauly says, waving his hand at the party. "But when the hell else are you gonna get the chance to work in such a high-class establishment as this?"

He has a point.

"They don't have a staff retention rate like mine at McDonald's." Pauly grins. "Fuck that place!"

"Fuck McDonald's!" Tyler yells, trailing toilet paper after him as he dances through the restaurant.

"And when these kids have families," Pauly adds, "may God save us all, they're gonna bring 'em here to eat."

Jai laughs at that.

A little while later, he catches sight of Devon leaning into Ebony's embrace at the counter. There's something a little too tender about that hug, given the madhouse they're in. He heads over.

"You guys okay?"

Ebony raises her eyebrows.

"Hey," Devon says, turning around to face him. "You talked to Nick today?"

"Yeah. Texted him earlier. He was thinking of coming but—" Jai looks around and shrugs. Then he catches Devon's expression. "Dev?"

"They're not talking," Ebony says when Devon clamps his mouth shut. "Nick's angry at Devon for telling his mom that he's been having panic attacks about college, and Devon's angry at Nick for *not* telling her, and now it's just a big ole fucking mess because neither of them are man enough to be the first to admit they need to hug it out."

"Wait. Nick's been having panic attacks?"

Devon nods. "He used to get them when he was younger. Like, he couldn't breathe and stuff. I don't think these are that bad? But now he won't tell me." He juts his chin out. "And before you say that he just needs to harden up or whatever, a panic attack is a legit thing, okay? They're not something he can just get over or whatever!"

"Yeah, that's not what I was going to say," Jai tells him.

Ebony pokes Devon in the ribs.

Jai grabs his helmet from beside the cash register.

"Where are you going?" Devon asks.

"To see Nick. I'll make sure he calls you."

Jai: *Italian meatball or chicken teriyaki?*
Nick: *I don't understand this question.*
Jai: *I'm bringing you a sub.*

Nick: *Why?*
Jai: *Because you can't eat pizza every night.*

"Hi," Jai says when Marnie opens the door. He holds up the Subway bag, swinging from one finger. "I'm here to see Nick."

Marnie opens the door cautiously, like she's afraid she may be letting an ax murderer into the house. Jai hopes it's just the motorcycle jacket.

"Upstairs on the right," she says, pointing to the stairs.

"Who is it, Marnie?" Chris calls from farther inside the house.

"It's Nick's—" She hesitates a little. "It's Jai."

Jai heads upstairs.

Nick's room looks like a disaster zone. It's everything Jai expected. It's crammed with comics and action figures, and there isn't a space on the wall that's not covered with some sort of poster. Lord of the Rings, Star Wars, Fall Out Boy, and a lot of stuff Jai doesn't even recognize. The fandoms run deep in this one.

Nick is sitting on his bed with a sketch pad on his knees and his laptop open in front of him.

"Brought you a sub," Jai says, and tosses the bag toward him.

Nick catches it against his chest. "Thanks."

Jai sets his helmet on Nick's desk, then sits down beside him. "Devon said you guys aren't talking."

"Yeah." Nick pokes at the Subway bag. "It's complicated."

"He's miserable," Jai says. "He also said you've been having panic attacks."

"Fuck," Nick mutters. "Is there anyone he *didn't* tell?"

Jai shrugs.

Nick opens the bag and unwraps his sub. He takes a bite, and lettuce rains down onto his sketch pad. "Shit."

He flicks a few pieces off onto his comforter.

"So, I was thinking—" Jai begins.

"Right." Nick says around a mouthful of sub. "Whatever."

"What?"

Nick swallows. "This is the part where you tell me that we're done in a few weeks anyhow, so we might as well call it off right now? Because I'm too weird and short and I have anxiety and I'm not very good at sex?"

"Wow." Jai raises his eyebrows. "Apparently both you and Devon think you can read my mind and predict exactly what I'm going to say next. Do you really think I would have brought you a sub if I was going to break up with you?"

Nick looks at him with his mouth hanging half-open, and then looks down at his sub, and then back up at Jai. "Um. I'm not really sure of the etiquette?"

"I'm not breaking up with you, Nick."

"Okay." Nick frowns. "Why not?"

"Because I like you," Jai says. "I like hanging out with you. I like making out with you. I even like it when I have something important to say and you totally manage to derail me. And what do you even mean that you're 'not very good at sex'?"

Nick flushes. "Um, because I can't last very long?"

"You're lasting a lot longer than you did the first time," Jai tells him.

"Really?"

"Yes. How can you not know that?"

"It's really hard to keep count of the minutes when we're fucking, Jai!" Nick counters, his voice rising. "I'm very easily distracted by your perfect ass and your incredible dick!"

Someone downstairs drops something breakable.

"Please tell me your dad doesn't have a shotgun," Jai whispers in the sudden, terrible silence.

Nick snorts. "Sorry. I've been told I have no indoor voice."

"Nick, I like sex with you, okay? And it's got nothing to do with how long you last. I like being with you. I think we've got something there, right?"

"Right," Nick echoes, wide-eyed.

"Good." Jai shakes his head and smiles at him. "Can I start this conversation again?"

Nick waves his hand and clears his throat. "Please."

"Okay, so." Jai reaches for the laptop and ignores the fact it's open at . . . Is that a cartoon boy being ravaged by something with tentacles?

Well, he seems to be enjoying it at least. Jai goes to Amazon. "So this is the backpack I ordered the other week."

Nick looks at the screen. "It's nice?"

"It is," Jai tells him. "It arrived a few days ago. Thing is, I already have a backpack. So I thought you might want this one."

Nick's eyes grow as large as the unfortunate manga boy's. "Um . . ."

"It takes three weeks to get a passport," Jai says. "And I know you have college money, right? Because, I promise, the biggest outlay is your airfare. Once that's done, we can get by on about sixty-five bucks a day each. A lot less if we pick up work as we go."

"Jai?" Nick's voice sounds tremulous. He drops his sub onto his sketch pad. "Are you asking me to come traveling with you?"

"Yes," Jai says. "There's a whole world out there, and I think you'd really love it."

"You . . . you want me to come to Argentina with you?"

"About that," Jai says, and opens a new tab in Nick's browser. "Not exactly."

Nick says yes.

Of course he does. He's the most impulsive person Jai has ever met.

It's a little harder to convince his parents. They've already written out the check to OSU, and they're not ready to tear it up straightaway. But better to tear it up now rather than wait until Nick begins classes. They won't see that money again if Nick starts school, makes it through a few weeks, and then crashes and burns.

"I don't want to make it like a threat," Nick tells them. "I really don't, but this is me. I mean, you guys, this is *me*." He looks suddenly horrified at the thought of his parents losing thousands and thousands of dollars on him, as though he's never before considered the depth of their investment in him.

And that investment, Jai sees, isn't just financial. Nick may think it is, but Nick doesn't notice the way his parents glance at one another, echoing back their worry.

"It's not something I can do right now," Nick tells them, swallowing. "I just can't."

"But you can travel to a completely different hemisphere?" Chris asks, a slight, wry twist to his mouth that Nick inherited.

Nick wrinkles his nose. "Maybe?"

Chris sighs, but the fight is leaving him.

And it's not a magical solution. It won't make Nick's anxiety vanish, but Jai really thinks that he'll thrive out in the world, as long as he's got Jai to make sure he doesn't walk into traffic or fall down a hole or whatever. And it gives him time to think about college some more. Maybe he'll want to go next year. Maybe he won't.

Maybe he and Jai will still be boyfriends, and maybe they won't.

But in a year, Nick will know himself more. Jai is certain of that.

The following afternoon, he turns up at Nick's house again and gives Nick the backpack.

"A backpack for ants!" Nick exclaims, delighted, and spends ages trying to figure out all the straps and clips and compartments. "Holy shit! Holy *shit*!"

His hands are shaking and his heartbeat, when Jai puts a palm over his chest, is rapid. But this isn't anxiety, exactly, even if his body processes it the same. This is excitement.

Jai and Nick sit down with Chris and Marnie.

Jai has detailed budgets. More detailed than they need to be, probably, but Chris Stahlnecker is a stickler for detail.

"My mom works in a bank," Jai tells him. "Ever since I got stuck once in Australia without any money, she's made me carry an emergency credit card linked to her account. That was three years ago, and I've never used it."

"Not even for emergency pizza?" Nick asks, astonished.

"Not even then."

Chris looks grudgingly impressed.

"I don't know," Marnie says faintly. "Nicky . . . this isn't what we *planned*."

"I know, Mom," Nick says. "But maybe I want to try this first?"

He sounds as nervous about it as she does, and Jai reaches out and laces their fingers together.

"I do," Nick says, more firmly this time. "I do want to try this."

Nick: *I've changed my mind. This is a disaster.*

Jai: *It's not. It'll be fine.*

Nick: *NO! IT'S A DISASTER OF EPIC PROPORTIONS!*

Jai: *Will a blowjob calm you down?*

Nick: *I don't know. Can we try it and see?*

The basement door slams open.

Nick squeaks and pulls his pants up.

"Oh, fuck you, Ronny!" Jai wipes his mouth with the back of his hand. "Again? Seriously?"

Ronny shows his palms. "Just thought you guys would want to know that Nick's parents are here."

Nick groans.

"Nice to see you again, Nick." Ronny grins.

"H-hey, Mr. Green. You too?"

"You can call him Ronny," Jai says.

"Because I'm eighteen and I've graduated, or because he's seen my dick?" Nick buttons his jeans. "*Twice.*"

Jai climbs to his feet. "All of those things, probably."

"Jai!" Nick flails. "My parents cannot meet your family. It's like matter meeting antimatter. It will be *terrible.*"

"It'll be fine."

"Jai! It could destroy the entire universe!"

"That's . . ." Jai leans down and kisses him. "That's probably not going to happen. You know that, right?"

"Yes!" Nick scowls at him. "Maybe? I mean, it *might*!"

Jai takes him by the hand and starts to lead him upstairs. "But it probably won't."

Nick sighs and squeezes his hand. "Okay, it *probably* won't."

Jai's counting that as a win.

The following night, Jai goes to watch a movie at Nick's place. Marnie lets him in, and tells him not to leave without the cookies she's made for his family. Chris wants to go through the budget again, but it turns out that what he really wants is an assurance that Jai's not going to dump Nick on his own on the other side of the world.

"No," Jai says in a low voice. "Whatever happens, even if we break up, I would never do that. I'll bring him home safe, I promise."

Chris nods, clearing his throat, and Jai realizes he just wants Nick to be okay. Jai misses his own dad suddenly, acutely, but then the sound of Nick's laughter from the kitchen takes away most of that sting.

So it takes a while to get around to actually watching the movie, and then Nick falls asleep before it's over.

Nick is adorable when he's sleeping.

So is Devon, who invited himself to movie night.

It's disturbing.

Jai takes his phone out, snaps a picture of them cuddled up like little snuffling puppies, and then lies down beside Nick.

If he can't beat them, well, what choice does he have?

Ebony: *OMG. They're ridiculous!*
Jai: *I know. How can we compete with that?*
Ebony: *I hear you.*
Jai: *You all packed for college?*
Ebony: *Yeah. My dad's driving me up tomorrow. Devon's not going until Friday.*
Jai: *You guys trying the long-distance thing?*
Ebony: *He keeps calling it that. I keep telling him 60 miles is not long distance. Not like halfway around the world! You're killing their bromance, you know.*
Jai: *I know.*
Ebony: *Are you smiling smugly when you type that?*
Jai: *Maybe a little.*
Ebony: *Are you guys all packed?*
Jai: *Nick has packed five times already. He's going to be in for a rude shock when I take out half the shit he doesn't need.*
Ebony: *Aw, you guys are going to have so much fun together.*

Jai: *We are. :)*

Ebony: *I already miss you guys, and I can't wait for next summer. Those pizzas won't make themselves!*

Jai: *Did Pauly ever get the olives out of the light fixture?*

Ebony: *Who knows? Anyway, you know Pauly.*

Jai: *Yeah, Pauly doesn't care.*

Ebony: *Good night, Jai :D*

Jai: *Good night. :)*

EPILOGUE

Three weeks later.

"**O**migod," Nick whispers, and his breath hangs in the air like mist before it dissipates.

The path curves a little as it climbs the hill. On the left, where the hill drops away, he can see a lake, and a large tree, and clusters of crooked chimneys. It's beautiful. In summer it must be a riot of color—he *knows* that it is—but it's still beautiful now.

It's *cold*. It's ball-numbingly cold. Last night Nick was complaining about it, and using it as a blatant excuse to snuggle with Jai for warmth, but right now he doesn't care. Right now he can't even feel it.

Because *holy fuck.*

He's not going to cry.

No. No, he is definitely not.

Jai grins and slides his arm around Nick's waist as they round the bend to discover the carved steps leading up to the round green door.

Nick stops, and two little girls run in front, giggling. Their parents are still leisurely dawdling up the hill behind them.

"Jai," Nick whispers. "Jai. It's *Bag End*!"

It's only a movie set. Nick knows that. He knows that it's not real, that it's just a foyer dug into a hill and that there's no actual dwelling behind that half-open door. But here he is, standing in front of Bilbo's house, on a cold New Zealand morning, and it's perfect. Everything is perfect.

Jai hugs him.

He doesn't say anything, and neither does Nick again.

He needs a while to process this, probably.

Like maybe thirty or forty years. That would do it.

It's not just Bag End.

It's Jai.

It's the way he suggested they go to New Zealand because he knew what being here would mean to Nick. And not because Nick's a hopeless fanboy. Not *just* because of that. But because Jai knows how important dreams are, and he wanted to show Nick that it is possible to chase them. It's the way Jai shrugged and said that Argentina would still be there next year, like it was no big deal to put Nick's dreams before his own.

Jai is incredible.

Also, they've been traveling for two weeks so far, and they haven't even had a single argument. That has to be some sort of record for people, right? It's probably because Nick is so mature and stuff now. Like, yesterday he saw this awesome plush tuatara that was as big as his head, and it was so impractical he actually thought twice about buying it.

He *did* buy it, but that's not the point.

Adulting. Nick is doing it right.

They take a lot of photographs, and Jai listens to Nick talk way more than is socially acceptable about Hobbiton, and then they head for the Green Dragon Inn for lunch.

In the afternoon, Nick falls asleep with his head on Jai's shoulder on the tour bus and doesn't wake up again until they're back in Rotorua.

"Thanks," he mumbles as Jai helps him not face-plant as he gets off the bus.

"For what?" Jai asks with a smile.

Nick kisses him. "Jai, for *everything*."

Dear ~~Devon & Ebony~~ ~~Devony~~ ~~Debony~~ Devebony,

New Zealand is AWESOME and I really wish you guys were here. How is college?

Today Jai and I went to Hobbiton and I might have cried it was so good. Tomorrow we are going to a brewery for lunch, because FUCK

YES the drinking age is 18! I may have to move here. Don't tell my mom I said that though.

I really miss you guys. Whenever I see something cool I want to tell you all about it, but you aren't here. So far I have only almost got run over once. I also had a cheese and pineapple sandwich. Like WTF is that about?

Miss you, and love you, and see you next summer!

Nick :)

Dear Reader,

Thank you for reading Lisa Henry's *Adulting 101*!

We know your time is precious and you have many, many entertainment options, so it means a lot that you've chosen to spend your time reading. We really hope you enjoyed it.

We'd be honored if you'd consider posting a review—good or bad—on sites like **Amazon, Barnes & Noble, Kobo, Goodreads, Twitter, Facebook, Tumblr,** and your blog or website. We'd also be honored if you told your friends and family about this book. Word of mouth is a book's lifeblood!

For more information on upcoming releases, author interviews, blog tours, contests, giveaways, and more, please sign up for our weekly, spam-free newsletter and visit us around the web:

Newsletter: tinyurl.com/RiptideSignup
Twitter: twitter.com/RiptideBooks
Facebook: facebook.com/RiptidePublishing
Goodreads: tinyurl.com/RiptideOnGoodreads
Tumblr: riptidepublishing.tumblr.com

Thank you so much for Reading the Rainbow!

RiptidePublishing.com

ACKNOWLEDGMENTS

Thanks to Amelia, for making me write it, and to J.A., Emma, and Sofia, my awesome betas.

ALSO BY LISA HENRY

Sweetwater
He Is Worthy
The Island
Dark Space (Dark Space #1)
Darker Space (Dark Space #2)
Tribute
One Perfect Night
Fallout, with M. Caspian
Fall on Your Knees (part of the *Rated: XXXmas* anthology)

With J.A. Rock
When All the World Sleeps

Playing the Fool series
The Two Gentlemen of Altona
The Merchant of Death
Tempest

With Heidi Belleau
Tin Man
Bliss
King of Dublin
The Harder They Fall

Writing as Cari Waites
Stealing Innocents

ABOUT THE AUTHOR

Lisa likes to tell stories, mostly with hot guys and happily ever afters.

Lisa lives in tropical North Queensland, Australia. She doesn't know why, because she hates the heat, but she suspects she's too lazy to move. She spends half her time slaving away as a government minion, and the other half plotting her escape.

She attended university at sixteen, not because she was a child prodigy or anything, but because of a mix-up between international school systems early in life. She studied History and English, neither of them very thoroughly.

She shares her house with too many cats, a green tree frog that swims in the toilet, and as many possums as can break in every night. This is not how she imagined life as a grown-up.

You can email me at lisahenryonline@gmail.com. Or check out my website at lisahenryonline.com.

Got Twitter? Follow me at twitter.com/LisaHenryOnline.

Hanging out on Goodreads? So am I: Lisa Henry.

Facebook: facebook.com/lisa.henry.1441

Enjoy more stories like
Adulting 101
at RiptidePublishing.com!

Poster Boy
ISBN: 978-1-62649-131-1

Lovers Leap
ISBN: 978-1-62649-383-4

Earn Bonus Bucks!
Earn 1 Bonus Buck for each dollar you spend. Find out how at
RiptidePublishing.com/news/bonus-bucks.

Win Free Ebooks for a Year!
Pre-order coming soon titles directly through our site and you'll
receive one entry into a drawing for a chance to win free books for
a year! Get the details at RiptidePublishing.com/contests.

CPSIA information can be obtained
at www.ICGtesting.com
Printed in the USA
FSOW01n2125150617
35271FS